MW01681350

Conversations with Sheryl Sutton

THE NOVEL OF A DIALOGUE

JÁNOS PILINSZKY

TRANSLATED BY PETER JAY AND EVA MAJOR

Conversations with Sheryl Sutton

THE NOVEL OF A DIALOGUE

CARCANET · CORVINA

First published in Great Britain in 1992 by
Carcanet Press Limited
208-212 Corn Exchange Buildings
Manchester M4 3BQ

In co-operation with Corvina Books
V. Vörösmarty tér 1, Budapest 1051
Hungary

Copyright © Corvina 1992
Translated from *Beszélgetések Sheryl Suttonnal*, 1977
Translation and preface copyright © 1992 Peter Jay and Éva Major

All rights reserved

A CIP catalogue record for this book is
available from the British Library.
ISBN 0 85635 868 1 (Carcanet)
963 13 3767 7 (Corvina)

The publisher acknowledges financial assistance
from the Arts Council of Great Britain

Set in Ehrhardt by Koinonia Ltd, Bury
Printed and bound in England by SRP Ltd, Exeter

IN MEMORY
OF
MY SISTER

ACKNOWLEDGEMENTS

We thank the British Council for travel grants which enabled us to meet and work on the translation, both in Hungary and in England; the Hungarian PEN Club for its encouragement, as well as additional financial support; András Szurdi for his hospitality which enabled us to work in peaceful surroundings at Lake Balaton; Tünde Vajda, formerly of Corvina Kiadó, for her detailed comments on the translation; and finally István Bart and László Kunos of Corvina, for commissioning the book and for their patience with its slow progress.

P.J., E.M.

CONTENTS

PREFACE

On the jacket of the first Hungarian edition of *Conversations with Sheryl Sutton* (1977), two notes in Sheryl Sutton's handwriting are reproduced. The first reads: "Dear János, I was very happy to read that you are working on 'our book'. It's evident that reality can be best approached only through fiction. I trust that our imagined dialogues are like those in life and I understand also that your book is not an interview but a 'novel of a dialogue'. I hope that your work progresses well. Love, Sheryl."

The second is on the back cover: "To János, From Sheryl the lady of the chair. Would that I could be as beautiful as your words. As the music of your language."

They met in Paris in 1973. Sheryl was there with Robert Wilson's company, performing in *Deafman Glance*. János was there because he was able to spend several months a year in Paris at Pierre Emmanuel's invitation. He had seen *Deafman Glance* before meeting Sheryl, by chance, in a café with her fiancé. They met again briefly a few times, and once for an extended meeting in which Pilinszky gathered many of the impressions and ideas that he later used in *Conversations*.

János Pilinszky described this book as a novel: "the novel of a dialogue" is its subtitle. This is important because readers might naturally assume that more of the book is biographical than is the case. (He also referred to it differently in the first chapter as "the only book of essays I am capable of writing"; and indeed the individual chapters are often essay-like.)

Pilinszky and Sheryl Sutton met only in Paris, and then only casually. Fictional though the framework, much of the detail and many of the stories told by János or Sheryl are, the book still captures something essential about their lives, manners, attitudes, and most of all ideas. But the book is also, most obviously and yet most profoundly, a love-story. The protagonists in this Platonic dialogue – one may use the term in both senses – share their ideas as they develop them.

Pilinszky chose Sheryl, it seems, as his muse for the purpose of writing this book, on the strength of the recognition, which she shared, of their affinity, spiritual and artistic. (Neither of them, I think, would regard those aspects as distinct from one another.) The fiction of her nursing him through his fever in Paris seems to me rather more than just a wry acknowledgement of his hypochondria; it is a metaphor of the healing power of art.

The Sheryl Sutton of this book is, of course, a fictional character. In some ways, she is Pilinszky's projection, persona or *alter ego*. It is not her at all, and yet it is her. But she has been truly imagined; the "real" Sheryl Sutton to this day subscribes to the artistic discipline which Pilinszky so memorably evokes. She also remembers Pilinszky with affection and admiration, as was clear from her tribute to him during the Barbican Centre's Hungarian Festival in 1989, when she took part in Patrick Garland's memorial programme at the Almeida Theatre.

The book is coincidentally a valuable treatise on what has come to be known as performance art. But its study of the creative imagination is more widely applicable, not least to Pilinszky's own poetry. The book dramatizes an internal debate about what kind of poetry he should write. As it happened, he wrote what proved to be his last poems, very much under the spell of *Deafman Glance*, during 1974–5, about the time he was writing *Conversations*. After 1975, he wrote only prose: another attempt at a novel, of which he left a few chapters, his regular newspaper column for the Catholic *Új Ember*, and other short pieces in prose. And yet the previous five or so years, from about 1970, had been extremely productive in poetry. This was the period when his style altered radically, from the austere and rigorously controlled strict forms which made his reputation, to the flexible free verse, with its tendency to the gnomic, of his later collections.

He was already on this path – one regretted by some Hungarian readers and critics, for whom his early poetry was incomparable – by the time that he encountered *Deafman Glance* in Paris. The performance confirmed his instinct that poetry – maybe poetry in general, but his own in particular – needed a new mode of addressing reality, and that Robert Wilson's emphasis on concentrated gesture and ritual was part of it. For Pilinszky, his new style brought both new possibilities of expression, and of subject. It prevented the kind of atrophy into repetition, or lapse into silence, which in quite different ways are deathly to the artist's purpose.

His later poems are often illuminated by this book. Several short poems from *Crater* are based on scenes from *Deafman Glance* described here. Even phrases from poems are repeated: "illuminated and forgotten". But although the book is closest in spirit as well as time to his later poems, it articulates the kind of spiritual struggles and values which are also at work in his earlier poetry. Despite the sharp contrast in style between his earlier and later poetry, there is no essential difference in thrust.

Conversations is an enigmatic work. The condensation of the writing in parts is extreme, and there are a few passages so baffling that nobody we have turned to has been able to shed light on them. We have not tried to simplify such passages in English. Pilinszky's syntax is idiosyncratic, almost improvised at times, matching the difficult and compressed nature of his thought, but he also uses ordinary words in special, personal senses.

We translated this book over the course of several years, meeting sometimes in Budapest, sometimes in Greenwich. It has been both a protracted struggle and a richly rewarding experience. There is a fascinating and unusual mind at work, and at the heart of Pilinszky's vision, a radiant clarity and faith in human life which triumphs over all the horrors, the worst horrors of the twentieth century, to which his memory constantly returned him.

Peter Jay

Conversations with Sheryl Sutton

THE NOVEL
OF A DIALOGUE

CHAPTER ONE

SHERYL SUTTON: I was born on 7th March 1950, in New Orleans, Louisiana. All my life up to now, neither being a woman nor being black has bothered me, and I've only very rarely been the leading character in my own life. I can give you three examples of this.

Back in New Orleans, there was a girl my own age, five or six, in the playground. She never joined in our games but always stood at the edge of the sandpit and moved only if a speck of dust landed on her clothes. I was playing with the others and as she stood there and moved, I played more and more wildly and eagerly to make her endure the fact that she both had to stand there, and move.

The next example I'll give is from the time when I got to New York as a fashion model, at the age of sixteen. The required starvation-diet broke me down both physically and mentally. I felt dizzy, I fainted, I forgot my name. I woke up to realize that I was in a mental hospital, lying in bed tense and helpless.

I didn't know what was wrong with me, just as I had no idea of my room-mate's diagnosis, either. All I knew about her was that she was an Austrian woman, born in Linz. Sometimes she lay on her back and stared at the ceiling, then she chattered excitedly, wandering up and down the room, and sometimes she gazed at herself in the mirror for hours on end, winding her nightgown around herself.

One morning she shook me from my sleep, full of hatred, saying that she had always loathed her husband and that she only married him on her mother's orders. "Now I'm in love with a pastry-cook!" she screamed, with hollowed eyes. "Money. Car. He's mad about me! I'm mad about him! My husband was religious and he would only ever come near me at night. When he died, I pulled the blanket off him. His genitals were *this* small – like this!"

For the first time in weeks I sat up in bed, and ever since then a grey, unfamiliar man has been lying on a mock-marble sarcophagus, with a stone veil wound about his loins.

My third story is perhaps the worst example. It happened in New York too, in my modelling days. I was having dinner in a side-room at a fashion salon, I don't recall who with; I remember a man with thinnish hair and a middle parting. I was drinking because they were making me drink, when the room opposite opened, and a yard or so from the piano, under the lamp stood a girl (a ghoul?) in a nightgown, in undone lace-up boots, until someone rushed in, slamming the double doors in her face.

The next day I went to a second-hand bookstore and spent hours rummaging through all kinds of photographs. A month later, when the phone rang in my hotel room, I couldn't make head or tail of the howling that came from the other end of the line, except that it was her talking with her lace-up boots undone, and standing with spread legs.

Exactly when I became an actress, I don't know. Perhaps when I learnt about the case of Eric Peterson from an article in a local paper. It was a long, distorted article but the facts of what had happened came through. Eric Peterson wanted to become a musician, and he had perfect pitch. His body was like a bird's, but his head seemed enormous, and even more so because it had such finely-drawn features. He was the one who for years had been carrying out the most notorious bank-robberies in New York. He actually demonstrated during the reconstruction how he caught the codes of safes with the aid of his exceptional ear. Peterson really didn't know what he was doing. Even in the daytime he never dared go out on the street by himself. Also, in the photographs taken during the reconstruction, he was kneeling between his two brothers, with his sister holding his hand. When I read the article, I spread the newspaper out on the floor and knelt on it.

Black families are big. I have ten siblings, five brothers and five sisters. Ted was always the most beautiful, but his eyes, as if they had never seen the world, reflected himself alone. I was just the opposite. My eyes weren't mirrors, they were an eternal absorption.

When I was eighteen, I entered the drama faculty at the University of Iowa. It took me less than a week to realize what a huge mistake I'd made. For me, acting is neither impersonation nor effect, but a kind of prison, a walled-in solitude where, fumbling around patiently in the infinite silence like blind people as they read, you pick that moment which forms first a letter and then, finally – perhaps – a rite.

Never in my life can I be so lonely as in certain roles. Then the audience comes up, first to the stage, and then I feel them gradually descending with me into that uncertainty which I was talking about just now.

Of course, with this belief I very soon fell behind the pack, but at least because of my helplessness and quietness my presence was tolerated, so that even if I wasn't taking part in rehearsals, I could stay and knit away in the armchair by the window. And there I was, like that, when Robert Wilson discovered me. For him then, a girl sitting, *the way she was sitting* – later he said I was sitting about there as heavily as a hundredweight – was the most important thing. In a word, I became an actress because with my ninety pounds even my jacket proved to weigh several tons. Wilson told me: I was sitting in such a way that I cut a crater in the earth.

Yes, and one more thing. My mother was the leader of a Protestant sect which is unknown in Europe. When I think of her exegesis, I understand the animal cult of the Hindus. Her commentaries hardly ever rose above the intellectual level of others, but every so often, I have to say, *it wasn't her who was speaking*. Her words were regularly followed by dancing and a feast. We tossed bananas and oranges into the air, and with our dancing, or rather our jumping about, we raised the dust to the ceiling. Afterwards at a stroke there was silence, we tidied our clothes, swept the floor and mopped up, after clearing the table which had been set in the middle – carefully laid but beyond recognition by now. Everybody was dead tired, but peaceful as animals who have found their way home for the night. Our black Christ died in vain on the cross, we blacks go on multiplying carefree like Jesus himself was anything but an only child.

Our fate, incidentally, is insoluble. In Harlem I was raped several times on the staircase by a boy much younger than me. I didn't see his face at first, just the vomit frozen like silver on his coat. Later I recognized him, and could only look at his face. When our paths first crossed in the street, I don't say that I felt he was good, but far better than the crowd milling around him. He was incredibly embarrassed, like a murderer just managing to hold himself together. But when I was clearing the wrecked table after our ceremony, I remember, I even gave him a name which I forgot in no time. The way he attacked me, his hunger and the risk he took excused him from everything in my eyes. Today I can't remember his face any more, just the silvery patch on his coat which is no different from the panting of the boy I've loved for years, and who I die with each time we've made love. He's white, I'm black. But by the time the pillow cools, there are no races left. We switch out the light and fall asleep, breathing in unison.

But I ought to tell you some more about my adolescence, too. Long after the war, my father, a black American soldier holding the rank of sergeant, served in Germany. I would have been ten or eleven around then. I remember that we lived in an eternally muddy, rainy village where the houses were scarcely different from the neatly-constructed stables. We lodged with a wealthy peasant. His garden was enclosed by such a high stone wall that the moon, for example, could only emerge when the whole house was already in bed.

A child's feelings are odd. Whether it was raining or not, I always felt that at a certain moment someone had unbuttoned the twilight. Mind you, I felt something similar about German women's dresses – especially young women's. There was a very beautiful girl, for instance, called Christine who dropped in on us almost every evening at lighting-up time, when the table had already been set. I liked the print-dress on this beautiful young girl so much, whether it was wet or dry, undone or done up, but most of all when it was done up and wet, that one evening when I couldn't get to sleep at all, I got dressed warily in the dark, slipped out of the house and stood in the rain. Then I committed the same thing again at least five or six times after Christine's visits. But what I can really only now understand is not what happened, but what didn't happen. How can I put it? Standing in the rain, I never for one moment thought of Christine.

But this still isn't exactly what I wanted to say about her. One time she came in the morning: the house was empty; the sun was shining bright; she had slippers on. She sat down in front of the window and was knitting away at something which she then handed to me, and which I then handled. Next the room began to stab, from the fact that Christine was there but mainly from the light, everything began to stab straight into my eyes. Even a Vermeer's brush couldn't depict that blessèd heaven, with me standing in front of Christine and looking at her, my eyes gouged by the migraine.

I want to end my life-history, I don't know why, in a seemingly arbitrary way, perhaps, by recalling this old memory.

Sheryl Sutton

— : I was born on 27th November 1921, under the sign of the Archer. They say that my left palm could easily be that of a common criminal, while the lines on my right hand signify order and some kind of talent.

Browsing through childhood photographs, so faithful to bygone reality – my sister held sway over me with a mermaid's beauty, while I in the calmness of subjection was growing up under her tutelage as undisturbed in the end as a hothouse plant that would otherwise die. Living it hardly was, but everything that people did to me, and most of all what went on around me, I sensed to the point of shivers.

My aunt was Mother Superior, so I spent most of my childhood among primitive nuns and juvenile prostitutes, half in prison and half in reformatory. A dress too loose or too short with its impersonality or, for example, with the fact that its wearer's hand or arm partly flops out of it, has ever since swept me into indescribable attractions. In my gapings, though, one element that can be called both personal and everyday may have been precocious. So many cuddling nuns or reformatory girls, who sometimes even burst loudly into tears – obviously not because of me – marked me for life. All the while, however, I just looked at the trees or simply the sun, without the slightest compulsion to understand.

My poetic inclination, developing alongside my adolescence, was completely different from the nature of my childhood. Here, on paper, I was engrossed in the *solution* for a while at least, and perhaps I'm only now beginning to realize that Sister Pia and Sister Alexia, or Krecsa and Micsicsák, by being with me without a beginning and cuddling me, then unexpectedly and irrevocably disappearing, presented me with almost the only alpha and omega of my life's increasing chaos.

Poetry for me is not a phenomenon beyond language, but rather one on the near side of language, or underneath language, in the same way that life remains underneath the wholeness of the universe. For me a poet is the kind of inhabitant of dungeons for whom the sheer sense of touch is more important than what he discovers by means of touching (think of Hölderlin and Don Juan), and he wants to encounter the wholeness of the world in such a way that he's all the more prepared to make do with what's left at the side of his plate. In the modern age I know of just four such artists. One is Dostoyevsky, Simone Weil is another, Witold Gombrowicz is the third and the fourth is Robert Wilson when he staged his work *Deafman Glance* ("Le regard du sourd").

Before the war my shyness, which from the outside might have looked pathological, had swept me from time to time into heretical attractions. Now as then, I neither regret this nor am ashamed of it. The war and the collective shock that followed, however, forced me back again, without my wanting it, to the common, the average run of life and of humankind within it.

The war was not something I lived through or suffered through: but it became mine. It gave me back the words of poverty and the touch of anonymous poets, together, of course, with the floor which usually wasn't enough even for sleeping.

It is an odd scandal and absolution of my life that its most direct shock was caused by Germans, while at one and the same time my mother herself was German. My father seemed like a First World War army officer, even in civilian dress. Every part of him, his hands, his feet, his forehead and his caved stomach, seemed so lonely, like the backs of some men when they are leaving home. But Mother was grove, orchard, till her death.

All my life, at least as long as they could cope with it, I was surrounded by crowds of beings. For instance, my old aunt who as a result of a childhood accident could hardly even learn to talk. As a child I tried to teach her but got nowhere with the exercise. Then once, weeks later, holding my face in her hands she uttered for the first time the word practised for days in vain: "tree".

My father was hewn from one block of stone, which explains both the goodness and the brutality that burst from him on occasion. He also had a few miserable precepts. He never laid a finger on my sister (who was older than me) from the age of ten, "because girls mustn't be beaten." Me he beat with all his might, indiscriminately. I've many times dreamed of his fist since then, both how it broke me to bits and how, with it clumsily open, he attempted to put me back in one such piece as I couldn't keep myself together in for ages.

I got to know Sheryl Sutton by chance in the spring of 1973. Her fiancé is a Hungarian boy, János Gat. When I was down with pneumonia in Paris she visited me every day, gave me food and drink, shook and plumped up my pillow. And she cooked for me. It was then that our ideas turned out not only to be parallel, but almost coinciding. Which is how the concept of the only book of essays I am capable of writing, *Conversations with Sheryl Sutton*, grew in me. Sheryl leaned back in the armchair and was doubled up with laughter for minutes when she heard this idea. Then she quickly got up and cooked the usual potato goulash for supper. We ate without praise, in silence. "I just have to think about the form of our book," I said, before she tucked me up to the chin, let some fresh air in and, after switching the light out, locked the door on me. I heard her go downstairs, then across the courtyard and out into the street.

I know she's not fond of me really, since women are rightly disturbed by sharp insight. Reduced as it is, she nevertheless needs some kind of stage, some field of play. Even she does. I hardly will, any longer. That's why I have to write her book for her, too. There won't be a word of untruth in it, but when she reads it, if she really finds it good and true, she'll soon commit something trashy. That's how it always is.

Such fine stories as the ones she told me about herself never happened to me. But I also suffered from migraine. Once when I was paraded with my whole school for the reception of the king of Italy, it attacked me for the first time. I've known since then that a king's path is a *single* granite flagstone – as if there were miles and miles that had been paved with *them*.

Now I'm skimming over twenty or thirty intervening pages of my life. The rest I'll attempt to tell later on, hidden behind code-words.

To Sheryl Sutton

János Pilinszky

CHAPTER TWO

On boredom – On time – Uncertainty as an indispensable quality

— : The most disconcerting experience of my adolescence was that the great novels are boring. Later – even before with my cloth ears I discovered Bach – I realized that masterpieces are beyond boredom, and not before it. What now disturbs me in modern literature is that it doesn't dare run the risk of boredom. I also know now that there's no masterpiece in which the author's failure isn't "built-in". This is actually the equivalent in art of unrealizable death. Even the finest genius creates *only* until his artistic and human failure is built into his work. From then on – without losing his hand's mark – the work begins to write itself, and this is one of those qualitative changes acting forwards and backwards without which even the masters would only remain the best students. Modern art, the art of our age, cannot avoid this bitter, murderous and suicidal element, which alone is redemptive.

But the trouble today isn't here, really. Almost all works stay on this side of boredom, are too "bare", too "bold", or simply too "loud" and "surprising" to venture into the zone where Tolstoy, Racine, Dostoyevsky and particularly Bach so naturally moved. They took a step which, apart from the monotony of rain, the live heart and so many other things, the sea, perhaps, in the most exemplary way is able to. There is no freedom and true greatness without conveyings beyond boredom.

SHERYL SUTTON: I would go further, myself. Quality is that which has no time. Among playwrights I think of Chekhov. Walking and standing about, that's what all his plays are. The comings and goings that there *are* in them, even those are just appearances. He brought what is beyond boredom directly to the footlights. He began where you need to yawn. His only tempo, his only measure of time is quality. Of course, this may have been his failing, too. He didn't dare bide time until still water, the cog-wheel that grinds up our lives, and restless emptiness lead to suicide or to maturity – or simply to running out of steam. In our age even the finest – I'm thinking of Beckett or Ionesco – didn't actually dare risk boredom. Built-in failure, they did. Their constant shifts make our minds if nothing else stand on their heads without cease. Beckett with the mirage of asceticism, Ionesco with the twists of the self-contained game, did not for a moment risk the danger after which and in the wake of which Bach so unerringly released the heart-beat of the sea or of a new-born baby. After what is beyond failure, almost the beyond-boredom richness and patience of plants.

It's in this that Robert Wilson excelled all his twentieth-century predecessors. Apparently simply by slowing down many times the movement of his characters. It wasn't either mime or slow-motion cinema. I would say it was a frank confession of clumsiness, all kinds of human clumsiness. A step five-times slow is also more beautiful, but much more ungainly and more perishable than the normal. The spell of slowed-down motion lay not in this, though, but in the revolutionary revaluation of time, of normal time. For, consciously or subconsciously, normal plays demonstrated just the opposite. At the usual speed of movement, they compressed the story of a whole life into three hours. Wilson managed to prove that with the help of movement slowed five times, he could present a much more condensed whole than the normal. So how and why, then? Because quality's time differs fundamentally from that of the alarm clock. Hölderlin told his whole life in four lines – and he had time enough for it. In so-called mimicry-drama the telephone rings, people knock, sit down, light a cigarette for exactly as long as in life. They too have time for it. For compressing commonplaces, even two hours are in fact a devalued eternity. Wilson's slow play, however, started such a process rolling as only the Greek tragedies were able, with their diction slowed to the utmost and their openness which from the outset destroyed action, to "utter".

The other virtue – theatrical virtue – of the play for me was the perfect isolation, the unpractiseable uncertainty of the movements which is derived from the slowness. Reaching one's hand out for a glass for minutes rules out all kinds of certainty. We used to fumble about blindfold like that once in childhood, searching for a hidden object or, with eyes open, for a fleeting playmate. And believe me, a hand that suddenly goes blind describes and feels out so much more in the air than any workman's unerring stroke with a hoe. Not to mention the fact that a play constructed with strokes is *meant to be* understood. About the boundless world, though, in which we all without exception live, you can only give a local, provincial "perspective". A blind man's movement, however, exempts you from all kinds of terror of this primitive stage-craft. It describes a thin, uncertain thread which the *whole* so clearly and openly, with no compulsion of solutions and explanations, keeps wafting about, making it float in nothingness and in the universe, just as only a new-born baby's eyes pierce last into the world.

Acting, in the standard sense of the word, has never existed and never will. Imitation is the nature of a few species of animal, and the impersonator's banter. The great artist's main task is to know nothing, over and over again. Only then can he repeat that extraordinary monologue which an infant carries on with a discrete object without any kind of easing from correlations. A child's monologue connects with the unceasing genesis of the world, while adults irretrievably make an effort to understand and to place things on the clever, easing but undoubtedly inferior level of correlations. Adulthood, if it can be called a success at all, lives in a widening range of constructions. An infant still looks at everything as itself and so, even without a *perspective*, knows a great deal more about *genesis* than do we, who can at least now talk about the local structures of the world. Knowledge is ours; babbling is theirs. But as long as an artist – be he a person of understanding and of correlations – is indeed an artist, he longs to know nothing over and over again, and with his intellect wishes himself back once more to that zero-point when alone it is worth taking the pencil in your hand.

All real art excludes all kinds of routine. Stammering is its alpha and eloquence its omega, but in such a way that it's impossible to separate one from the other and to distinguish between them. The exclusive mark of this "style", of course, is that it should be *blind*, like Homer. That is to say, a style which truth might have blinded with its own hand. Oedipus Rex.

Perhaps I should give just one example now of what I feel is the inevitable failure of "mimicry-theatre". If someone is not telling the truth, and is really not telling the truth, he can't cover it up with any kind of acting. It's obvious from this that the kind of acting I have in mind always comes into being in the blind, the deaf and motionless centre of things. How, then? – More about that next time.

CHAPTER THREE

Sheryl tells me off – Two hours' sleep – The role of the moon and the sun – Aggressive drama and the stage of silence

SHERYL SUTTON: No, please don't go on! I can see that my look embarrasses you with its frankness, but believe me that's no virtue of mine but of generations. From your very first word I've known what you want to talk about. Sin: your sins. Well then, let me tell you something. In New York, at a matinée performance, standing with her back to the wings as if she had been standing there since time immemorial, a girl of about eight caught my eye. She wasn't beautiful, I'm sure, but she made me tremble to the core. You mustn't – I kept repeating to myself – you mustn't go anywhere near her. At the end of the performance, though, I still went to her dressing room. I know now that it wasn't really her that attracted me, but the act itself, yet I still didn't want to commit with her that thing after which the most elementary abandonment – without which there is neither sin nor thought, role nor repentance any more – would have ceased in me. What happened to me later, however, was even more direct than this. I was staring at an old woman in a restaurant until, under the table opposite, she spread her legs. This isn't pornography, you see, but a kind of communion in which you receive nothing on your tongue-tip. True, we're all nothings but it's just this nothing which we mustn't reduce to nothing. Both these cases gave me the impression of wide-awake fainting. Embracing anyone since then has been a feeble copy of those two hells. And now, let me crochet and you take a short nap before lunch. You, after all, said we were going to talk behind code-words. About theatre, poetry, one thing and another. And it's not glossing over, on the contrary it's confessing things. If we get to our real ideas, a single half-sentence of yours will be enough for me to understand much more about you than anything that can be put in words. But now you should rest until lunch, and if you must think about something, then what about why this Sheryl endlessly crochets pink hats and scarves? I can feel from your forehead that the medicine is beginning to work already. Shall I close the curtains more? I can see quite well with them parted like that. No, no. I won't go into the other room while you're asleep.

— : What's the time?

SHERYL SUTTON: It doesn't really matter, you got at least two hours' sleep. I think you should read for a while. It's behind you, on the floor.

— : You're mistaken; I feel perfectly fresh. Where did we break off? Let's take the sun and the moon, for example. Together with the seasons, these two celestial bodies are the usual means of compression without the play switching into another rhythm. What's more, the words you meet in it are generally much more correct than brief conversations in life. With Wilson, however, the sun doesn't indicate time, it simply rises in its grandeur, it is *there*, as it is in sentences of great poetry. He doesn't need the moon for the fact that it's grown dark. Rather, in a Watteau-like way: its presence impinges on the gestures of young infantas and perhaps also the white piano on which a big black girl was playing Chopin. Remember? It all began in a lit-up auditorium, on a set enclosed by a wall, with a murder fit for a rite, before which you drew on elbow-high black gloves, then with a white veil covered the boy whose throat was slit with a razor. I can see you much more clearly now than I could then. The sheet became red and you were about to leave when another boy, the same age as the one you killed, blocked your path in a spasm of vomiting. The stone wall runs up and the thicket of lights in the auditorium goes out. Thereupon you and the other – beyond the stone wall running up – enter, enter the park dreamt up by Watteau and

Chopin: two irreconcilable beings into the illogic of the incalculable ambience of sin and dream. The moon, the round, silver and terrifyingly strong moon, I need hardly perhaps say, was not measuring time even in the Chekhovian sense here. It's an example of how the world, despite all appearances, is not a warehouse-like mass of either space or time, and particularly not of facts, but genesis.

Would you bring me a glass of water?

SHERYL SUTTON: What really got me attached to Wilson's theatre was silence rediscovered. As opposed to the Living Theatre or the increasing aggressiveness of modern German theatre, I daren't go so far as to say that Wilson has found the last word. I've already talked of the unbridled high spirits and the unfamiliar Jesus of our Protestant gatherings. When I think of a really new theatre, though – my ideal is the Catholic mass. The star-like movement of the priests, the childish discipline of the acolytes and the beautifully embroidered clothes themselves. In a word: that clear contradiction through which alone it's possible to contemplate what was perhaps the world's bloodiest drama. Only in Auschwitz have I seen anything comparable to this. On the walls of a long corridor, stamp-sized portraits of a million criminals, full-face and in profile. At the end of the corridor, though, the photograph of an angel-faced SS soldier. He was their murderer. Art is a change of places, in one way or another. The justice-dispensing changing of places of illusion and reality. Wilson is still only scratching the surface of this; but me, as I knit away in front of the window, I can dimly make out more and more as the pink holes gather and slide down my knees.

— : I felt something similar in Tours, at a performance of Berio's *Labyrinth*. It's a masterpiece in a certain sense, but every sound in it is mixed from effects. The following day I heard a Mozart serenade, also conducted by Boulez. Pure discipline, convention if you like. Still: you feel the finger of a diagnostician with a dead-sure touch, who the moment he has palpated the fatal point, withdraws his finger as he at once knows everything. He adjusts his ruffled sleeves, the patient is bolstered up, and the promenade music goes on as it always has.

To this degree Wilson is not Mozart. But who among us is? One things remains certain: he succeeded in drawing back from provocative theatre into silence. I suspect that the end of the millennium will go off in the spirit of merciless criticism. On stage – if nowhere else – Wilson re-established the beyond-boredom period of silence and beauty.

SHERYL SUTTON: You're tired now, I can see. And there are still so many things we should talk about. I'll slip down before the shops close.

— : No, don't go, only if you're hungry.

SHERYL SUTTON: We all have to eat. Just a few words quickly, anyway. In Paris I was at a Greek Orthodox Easter service. The trees in the garden were festooned with coloured lights, just as we do in America. The worshippers assembled in an undisciplined way, chatting as if in God's stable. The iconostasis was closed but there in the middle was Christ's coffin and a sacred picture, grubby from being kissed by everybody. The rite itself went off in a remarkably disciplined way except when the priest tore open the door of the iconostasis, and bellowing inarticulately in his resplendent cope, ran round the congregation which made way for him. He kept howling: "Christ is risen." Then from hand to hand we lit the melting candles in our hands, and kissed each other on both sides of the cheek. You see, with the closed character of the rite but with its human exuberance at the same time, it brought me closer to Wilson again. But more about this after dinner. Give me a few francs, please, if you can, for oranges, butter and bread. Don't get up, nobody's going to come anyway. It'll be all right to leave the door open.

CHAPTER FOUR

Bearing and birth – Circus and arena – Illusion

SHERYL SUTTON: You're better really now. It's past ten o'clock and you're still sleeping like a log. Wake up, d'you hear?

— : Do you know what heaven it is to drop from nearly 104°to 96.5°? The medicine ruined my gut; nothing but a good strong cup of tea! Come over here now and sit on the side of my bed.

In 1965 chance so ordained it that I *had* to talk with Dürrenmatt for an hour at least. (Both in its allusion and meaning that verb in the past tense refers rather to Dürrenmatt than to me.) I even took a photo of him with his chained cockatoo. Our meeting was a so-called official visit, but I've never been able since to get one of his remarks out of my mind. He said that the stage is a kind of condensed space in which every entrance has the value of giving birth. Whereas in the cinema – because of its technical ease – everyone is simply *there*, without any screen birth-throes.

SHERYL SUTTON: Word by word this is true, but it doesn't hold good for *Deafman Glance*. Wilson always gives a simultaneous exhibition, and so you only notice that an actor has entered when he has been on stage for some minutes. In this he was copying not the "ease" of film but the nature of human encounters and interaction. By the time you're aware of someone, he's been in the middle or at the end of his fate for ages.

But what Dürrenmatt said about the joy and sorrow of giving birth onto the stage, with Wilson was shifted to the bitter struggle of the most vulgar change of places. Having risen from my throne a good half-hour into the first act, I was sweating from it. It wasn't that I made an entrance, but that I made any movement at all. I can give you thousands of similar examples. Dürrenmatt speaks of entrance for when Wilson makes a paralysed person move, or even conjures non-existent creatures from nothing, in the same way that we're unable to cut back a single speck of dust or, same thing, the universe to the phenomenon of bearing-birth. Wilsonian drama was not born in the too easy-seeming magic of film technique, but from an astonishment greater than this bearing-birth I've just mentioned, from the fact that what is incomprehensible simply exists, and exists here. With Wilson we are never lost in wonder at the fact that something has happened, or that someone has entered. Our wonder is much deeper than that. What we admire is not that something has been born, but that it exists at all. But of course his theatre has its own characteristic technique. It reminds me of circuses and arenas. Barnum's circus has always shown several acts at the same time, just as athletics meetings happen in the plural, simultaneously. So, fairly or unfairly, the wandering and divided attention is always condemned to what is most important. To what is even more important than giving birth and "entrance". To what, then? To the simple presence of the world, to that single point where deception is impossible, to that miracle which little by little only children, lunatics, saints and imbeciles are engaged in, mind and eyes.

CHAPTER FIVE

Fehérvár – Letters, articles, index-cards – My sister – New York – Sheryl arrives at last

— : I'm asleep, or rather I'm just dreaming. Sometimes I'm twenty years old, sometimes thirty. I have fair hair and I wear glasses. I'm sitting at the front of the class, where I've never sat. My nails are clean, like my exercise books. And of course I'm taking notes, which I never did. My favourite authors: Jules Verne, Karl May and a guide-book.

I'm afraid of girls, and so I have plenty of time. I fill out index-cards, write articles and correspond, mainly with Dutch and American universities. For the last ten years I've been going to write a history of New York.

I've never been successful with women. They get scared at what I might want from them. I'm past fifty-four now, and my sister fifty-six. I have only to look at her to realize what she lived through for five years, until in the end, half-undressed, she died. Her face is grey dough, her nightgown plastic.

My index-cards are suffocating. But I'm making an effort. My glasses are on the little table; I receive visitors; I'm drinking and I'm on sleeping pills.

I'm not asleep, I'm dreaming. I was past fifty-four when my sister ended her life in the next room. For weeks, for months my letters festered unopened on the armchair pushed against my bed. Still, I've managed to get one open: it was an invitation from Columbia University. I've become an expert, they know who I am. After five weeks I finally have a bath, wash my hair and get a haircut. My two old aunts get me dressed, we go out to the airport, and I board the machine. I eat what they put in front of me, as we gradually begin to descend.

On the American plane I'm altogether more alert. My first

observation is that they have no sense of form. The seats are comfortable but are nothing in particular, like the great sins for a short while. Everything is flower and plastic, Swedish loneliness in ice-cream colours, though for the first time the stewardesses aren't models as on the continent but preoccupied student girls. Their efforts make them wrinkle their foreheads, but when – very rarely – they burst into giggles, it's always all of them at once.

We land in Boston, near the sea. From here we're taken to New Haven, to a large villa, where I spend weeks in a kitchen fit for a drawing-room. I have an aversion to the long-haired cat, but it's good that the Siberian dog is here, good too that he's forever following me and looking at me. One of his eyes is golden-brown, the other blue.

From New Haven we go to New York by car. From right or left, no view. Dry meadows and gravelly fields. Then in the midst of thick weed, a flat, snow-white factory. Not a man or a car to be seen. No smoke, no cables, no wires. In a blue-covered copybook which I've brought all the way from Fehérvár, I write my last entry in thick letters: "Snow-white row of buildings. Worse than everything perhaps. Sing-Sing, with no guards or prisoners. The concentration camp of pure material."

New York – Manhattan. We run on broken-down roads and soaring highways. The air, like a dusty glass window; behind it, we fall, rise and mark time at the height of the midriffs and tops of houses red as cattle-blood. Every third house is burned out. Torn curtains in windows, a black man in yellow boots, a blue hussar-type jacket and crimson Velasquez-hat on a balcony. Him I see looking upwards from below; a grey-haired woman lounging on a striped eiderdown, downwards from above. The shop-fronts are boarded up. A boy in a winter coat, shivering with cold and glued to the dog-days-deserted corner.

Dante was still thinking in circles, Manhattan is a square-ruled copybook page. Avenues and crossroads, signposted with numbers instead of names. After Harlem the luxury district of skyscrapers, with some touchingly overgrown art-nouveau buildings. But since New York is a biblical city, you get the same radial effect from any point in it. New York is everything that comes to your mind. Skyscrapers like giants: even more delicate beings than flamingoes. At dawn they are blue, at nightfall pink. Their size at best merely makes the streets intimate. Even in the daytime, the shops have atmospheric lighting. Only people with urgent business go out on the street. Everybody's in a hurry without reflexes. My hotel room is covered with a yellow carpet which the sunset just makes even more yellow. It's good to stroll barefoot on it. Still, after a few turns in the room I start to hurry without reflex, as I never do on grass. All my work has been useless! This city hasn't got, can't possibly have a history! Without antecedents it has grown from under the earth, from nothing.

I go to sleep and wake with a start. Where can Sheryl be? I can't get to sleep. Then I dream that I'm waking up. Unbelievable how many antique shops there are in this city with no history. I've time to spare until eight o'clock; I drop at random into one of the second-hand bookstores, and begin to rummage among the oldest papers and photographs. All pictures from the last century. The top part of one of the loveliest must have been fogged, so you can only see a bed and a woman's hand with a dangling handkerchief.

You're here at last! You don't know how I've been looking forward to seeing you.

SHERYL SUTTON: You've got a temperature again.

— : Sheryl, our book has helped me plan the idea for another book. I hardly dare admit that it might be a novel . . . hold on, I'll tell you where it's got to so far.

SHERYL SUTTON: Not bad. Of course, everyone and no one is a New Yorker. More precisely: someone who's never been there can be a New Yorker, and you can live even a hundred years in New York without ever knowing where you've been living.

— : Never mind my temperature. Don't you understand me? First time you've not understood me? But it was you who said that art is neither reality nor imitation. That the trouble's exactly this – that reality can only be imitated. Yet the essence of reality is that it never imitates anything. It simply is, or has its genesis. Then you also condemned mere invention. Because for *genesis* pure invention is just as much an imitation as is copying things that exist. I remember exactly, that's just where you drew the front line between continental and Anglo-Saxon art of today. "Art is nothing," you stubbornly reiterated, with dialectics weakeningly reinforcing each other, "but *the invention of reality*." We can't create and we can't copy reality. But creative invention involves the unavoidable similarity and the indispensable creative element. That's why we might now feel that Francis Bacon's figures lolling on the toilet, the never repeatable and illuminated concreteness of human flesh, may be even more abstract than the most successful abstractions.

Well: I have imagined a New York novel which is the novel, on the one hand, of everything that comes into my mind, and on the other . . . But where shall I continue? For me there's a crucial difference between structure and model. Structure is perhaps the final detective-work of mankind's nihilism straining for absolute certainty. Macrocosm and microcosm have slipped into the hands of natural scientists. Their teenage-like daydreams justifiably make the philologer-philosophers nervous about their glass-bead game. Microcosm and macrocosm cannot be viewed from the *outside*. How much easier a business structure is, which – even against a criminal dragged back to a reconstruction – shrinks the whole bounded and boundless world to material proof.

As opposed to this, the word "model" is both older and more modest. I think of Greek, romanesque and gothic churches. They all differ from each other, but they are still all authentic and valid models of the boundless whole.

The model has some significance beyond itself, but points

towards the object beside which it is dwarfed. Structure: a country banker. Model: a maid faithful until death.

Do you understand me now? I'd like to write New York in twenty or thirty models.

SHERYL SUTTON: You've got a temperature again, and you've gone and broken the thermometer.

— : Tell me, Sheryl, would you allow me at last to tell you who I really am?

SHERYL SUTTON: I will. But don't you ever write it.

CHAPTER SIX

The first act

— : For those who have not seen Robert Wilson's play, I feel that it's time I attempted to relate *Deafman Glance*, as I saw it.

*

Seashore, shingle, noise of gulls. Sheryl, as in an Edgar Allan Poe poem, is sitting in a throne-like armchair in the full light of noon with a black raven to her left. Her dress, cut from black taffeta, is ground-length and motionless.

*

Before I knew her, a few weeks after the performance, I even wrote a poem on this sitting-about. Ted Hughes made an English translation of it. Here is the original:

BŰN ÉS BŰNHŐDÉS

Sheryl Suttonnak

A befalazott képzelet
még egyre ismételgeti –

A pillanat villanyszék trónusán
még ott az arc
sziklábamártott nyakszirt
gyönyörű kéz –
pórusos jelenléted.

Még tart a nyár.

Ereszd le jogarod, Királynő.

Ted Hughes's translation, I feel, captures in English the same black American girl of whom I, a Hungarian, took my snapshot. Sheryl found the poem dedicated to her nice, though a bit overexposed.

CRIME AND PUNISHMENT

The walled-in imagination
continues to repeat it –

the face is still there
throned in the electric chair of the moment
the nape dipped in cliff
the beautiful hand –
the porous skin of your presence.

And still the summer goes on.

Let down your sceptre, Queen.

*

A runner runs across in front of the sea from time to time, like the whimsical pendulum of a metronome. Ancient runner, in satin shorts. But it's also possible that with his unexpected metrics, with his appearing, he is following the beat of a cantata even more heavenly than Bach's. He holds a baton which as he runs from right to left and left to right he never gives, never can give to anyone.

On the sand at first a naked human couple is dancing, Adam and Eve, perhaps, before the fall. Then the stage-hands pull a prehistoric turtle on a thick leash across the set, directly in front of Sheryl's chair, when a child comes and begins to play in the sand. Then an old married couple, brokenly. From the programme I learn that this is Freud and his wife. They approach Sheryl, then turn back at a loss. Next a cheerful black man padded fat and dressed in white pirouettes in shouting noisily, with a black mosquito net on his head, but no sooner has he disappeared than a sackcloth descends in front of the sea. Brown at first, then cattle-blood red, then golden-brown like the New Haven dog's left eye. There's a cut-out the size of a door in the sack curtain. By this time you can no longer see the sea, only the runner's legs, arms, baton unexpectedly appearing and disappearing in the cut-out.

It is becoming completely dark. From high above the stage dangled a clumsy little table, the kind you get in front of windows in cheap hotels. Its four small legs hung senselessly in the stage's brightness and its twilight. By nightfall you can't see it any more, it even slips out of your mind.

Sheryl continues to sit motionless, when for the first time in the play a human voice emerges. It is very soft, very girlish. "One-two-three; one-two-three; one-two-three . . ." From the left, a giant black girl with yard-wide padded breasts and buttocks comes waltzing in on stilts, and suddenly stops behind Sheryl. Silence. "One-two-three. One-two-three. One-two-three . . ." The voice is distant, intimate. From the right, a black midget woman in black taffeta, with upraised little arms shorter than stumps and padded top and bottom a yard wide, spins in. The giant and midget black girls stand motionless facing each other behind Sheryl's back. The *darkness* is unbearable. "One-two-three; one-two-three . . ." From the left fifty and from the right fifty clumsily spinning black girls, their movements a jumble, padded from shoulder to ankle. An atmospheric lamp in one of their hands. She shunts and pulls its white flex with a bitter struggle among unskilled legs and metal-studded heels. We are struggling as in a dream until at last the atmospheric lamp bursts into light. Then Sheryl stands up and, without beginning to tremble, breaks out into a sweat.

Zzzzzzzzzzz: the small hotel table lands. Sheryl gets as far as the table and, with tremendous agony, wants to take something off it, and would like to put it back.

CHAPTER SEVEN

"Modelling"

SHERYL SUTTON: Let's do some "modelling"! I'm a fifty-four-year old teacher from Székesfehérvár; I'm on the twentieth floor, walking comfortably barefoot on the yellow carpet which is yellower still in the light of the dipping sun, when I suddenly start to hurry. All my work has been useless!

— : But that's *me*, in fact!

SHERYL SUTTON: So what's the difference? It was your idea, and you can't understand it? Anyway, I take my pyjamas off and get dressed correctly, the way I grew accustomed to in Central Europe. In the elevator-mirror I've time to check my moustache, the parting in my hair and the alum-staunched cut under my chin.

Dusk comes separately to every street, every square.

"Name?"

"Sheryl Sutton."

"Nationality?"

"Hungarian."

"At your service!"

The building is grey and on a discreet copper plate is the one word: Ambassade. In the first courtyard a lawn, some trees and closed windows. Only the rusty iron semi-circle in the well-kept grass strikes the eye: "Arbeit macht frei." ("Work sets free.") It might have got here from one of the German reception camps, they could have just thrown it on the ground. But it might even have been manufactured here.

The second is the really interesting yard. Girls in outgrown clothes sweep leaves around, without sweeping them up. The embassy's inner building is prison and convent. Just now a sexless nun hands the gift to the prelate sitting at the head of the table.

Prelate: How many girls, how many blind people, how many sisters must have knitted this coat day and night? Thank you, I love it already. It isn't white the way snow is, but like a lime-pit. The devotion of my girls has discovered the very holes to keep me alive still. Please, help me on with it . . .

Mr Környei from Székesfehérvár! Take a seat, sir, please, and you too, Miss Sutton . . . and let us be patient. On the second floor of the convent, Mother Superior is in her death-throes. She is still alive at the moment. But in a short while there will be candles lit in every window.

Open the ground-floor gate, please! Can you see? Eric Peterson is kneeling in front of the safe. But at my special request his old mother, not his brothers, accompanied him here; she keeps handing him tools from a fish-bag. Look at that, the safe is now pure gold. I especially asked Peterson to do it barefoot. Can you see how beautiful he is now? More beautiful than Mozart or Bartók.

Don't anyone, please, sit there! Those two places are reserved for him, for after work. For him and for his mother. Sister dear, bring Peterson some fish, but nothing for the old woman, it's enough for that one that she clutches the bag.

The windows are ablaze! It's hard for me to scrape the oranges out from under the snow-laden table. Peterson, please take a seat!

This is Sheryl Sutton here, this is Mr Környei from Fehérvár, Eric Peterson and his mother and some enchantingly beautiful juvenile prostitutes leaning on brooms or craning their necks and wrinkling their foreheads at the end of the table. More beautiful and more perishable even than Peterson. It's a scandal that I can still see the world with lizard eyes!

At this point the prelate started to talk about his crocheted coat again. I organized things so that I could be next to Peterson. Was he executed in the end? I didn't want to ask him. His mother took my hand. The old creature was hardly alive now, but ticking. Could she believe that Peterson was a man? I did my best to prevent her sensing that I was a girl.

— : You've really got into it, I can see, so let's carry on "modelling"!

SHERYL SUTTON: The *Prelate* : Our Mother is dead. The holes in my coat are mine, now and for ever. Who among the reformatory girls could take her place? – Nobody, then. Peterson? Sheryl? Mr Környei? – I expected this silence. From tomorrow on, we will close the top two floors.

Hand me a broom, girls, and one of you who would like to, would she sit at the head of the table! Mr Peterson, you've worked magnificently today. When you found the code, your head was Bartók's, and the safe a tabernacle. Head and box: pure gold.

Sheryl, it's your fate alone that I can't see. Will you permit me to call you Sheryl? If you wish, you may even stay here forever, and you will be one of the most beautiful, nunlike prostitutes. No one will be jealous of you, Miss Sutton, I'm sure. Look at Micsicsák's freckles; can there be anything like it? Look at Krecsa's frozen hands; is there anything more embarrassing? Or look at Christine's – she was sitting at the table just now? Is there a dog that departs more beaten than this surpassingly beautiful girl?

It's not my lizard eyes that ask you to stay. You know too, Miss Sutton, that New York . . . it doesn't matter between us, who's who, even. Well then, I stir the leaves all day and Krecsa sits at the head of the table, looking for a banana for Mother Superior in her death-throes or for a new guest such as you, for instance.

Today exceptionally a candle burns in every window; Peterson has fallen asleep on his mother's shoulder; Arbeit macht frei . . . Someone may have thrown it into our garden, and so perhaps you'll understand and forgive that we can't do any more with it than let it rust.

Go away, my girl! Don't stay among us!

CHAPTER EIGHT

In a Victorian drawing-room – Before the wall, after the wall – Outside-inside – Supper at the Frog-King's – The day of wrath and the apotheosis of the characters

— : Sheryl had me confused for a moment, she dragged me into my own "game", while in fact there are intervals in the theatre too, and it makes no difference then what we're chatting about.

Before I continue with my account of Wilson's play, though, I must reveal that the play had another glaring formal feature besides the slowed-down movement. Apart from a few sentences, the performance of several hours was given by the characters mute. But like their slowness, their dumbness seemed natural too, the way trapeze artists don't speak, either. Unlike most European avant-garde endeavours, it seemed rather to confirm an old commonplace. Namely that the poetic word in its essence is a speaking silence, compared to which all else is idle backchat. Or rather: the presence of poetry is the huge silence on stage that cannot be rendered dumb by any word.

So I continue with my description of the second act. Drawing-room skinned to tobacco-brown; the door-sized cut-out in the wall at just the same position as in the first act, but in the "recurrent" cut-out *now* a blazing wheat-field. In the drawing-room which at first seems perfectly and for years abandoned, the actors arrive one after another through a visibly curved corridor (hall? gateway?). Nowhere a door which they have to open or could knock at.

The first guest: a middle-aged salesman-type. Apart from the worn seat of his trousers, there's nothing conspicuous about him. He can't go directly to the game-table since he first has to go round the huge folding screen placed in mid-stage. The salesman stops by the small game-table.

Second, fumbling around with his white stick before him, a blind man turns onto the stage. He too goes round the screen in the middle. So now there are two of them, standing beside each other. They stand for minutes, when one of them picks something up from the small table and moves it further away. Then in a few more minutes, the other stirs and moves something further away, something prepared in advance. They begin to play.

Third a young man in black, with a red bunch of roses in his arm. He places the bunch on an upholstered armchair. He lights a cigarette, and plunges into the other two men's play. He watches the game but takes no part in it himself.

Young girl in an evening gown: She picks up the bunch of roses, intended for her as it happens, and is about to sit down. The armchair moves from under her. Again she makes as if to sit down, but the armchair again moves. The girl stays standing, doesn't sit down. The armchair stays. The girl sits down in the armchair.

Old lady: Everything about her is so bare and over-drawn that in her greyness she strikes one as even more square-shouldered than the indifference of the most beautiful gold-soaked swimming girls. She steps straight to the bar-counter, fills her glass, then sits down in the corner next to the entrance. She has already been sitting there for minutes, when the glasses on the bar-shelves clink together.

In the game it should now be the blind man's turn, but the young man dressed in black goes instead, then all three change places.

Milkmaid in gumboots: She herself doesn't know how she got here. She stops in embarrassment right by the screen.

Grey gentleman with mouse-like steps: Fills his glass, then sits down in front of the tall piano propped against the wall. He stands his glass on top of the piano. What is he waiting for? The glasses on the counter delicately clink together. The man begins to play, very softly and interminably. It seems now that he was playing the first movement of Bach's *Well-Tempered Clavier*, formed into perpetual motion.

Then three arrive at the same time: *a young man, a careworn old woman and a young girl.* A briefcase in the man's hand. He takes a sheet of paper from it and gives it to the old woman, who passes it on unread to the young girl. But she doesn't read it either; just the milkmaid, then the piece of paper passes from hand to hand, until the young man finally locks it back in his case.

Ssshhhh – Ssshhhh – Ssshhhh – Ssshhhh: From the corridor a seal of enormous bulk heaves itself in. Struggling, swelling and rippling all over the place, it settles at last in front of the screen and begins to fan itself with a tiny fan.

Meanwhile in the door-sized cut-out, the wheat-field has disappeared. In its place can be seen an oared vessel, a sort of ancient storeyed galleon with banks of slaves, long oars, in post-diluvian peacefulness and security.

From the left two old-German peasant girls wearing frieze carry hay in and stack it up in front of the game-table. In gold bundles they carry the hay on wooden forks; they themselves, as their strong backs and manner of movement attest, are servants of a vanished golden age.

Then in front of the haystack a black girl on stilts, breast- and buttock-padded a yard wide, sings an unrestrained spiritual.

From the right a small group stealthily smuggle a ladder into the scene and, in the silence that sets in, place a naked dead body at the top of the ladder. The pianist goes on playing the temporarily suspended but unending melody, and the seal drags itself from in front of the screen to the haystack. As soundlessly as they placed it on, the small group remove the dead body from the ladder and slowly begin to move off with it. Everyone in the drawing-room gets up from their places and joins them. The scene is becoming empty again, for years or decades. We even forget the seal's presence.

There are those who are ready to start clapping now, when

a low whine rises to the pitch of a full howl, and from behind the screen a creature grown to no more than four and a half feet bursts forth and begins to rush at the spectators.

In the course of one of my conversations with Sheryl Sutton I have given a partial account of the third act. I should still like to repeat the whole act now, filled out with other, new motifs, as it also repeats itself again and again in me, if only because this scene was the play's obvious raw material.

The scene starts in a lit-up auditorium, indicating that we commit our most hidden acts out in the open, in the limelight; that is, in such a silence and loneliness as in the very centre of an overcrowded arena.

The stage – for this period – is blocked with an enormous brick wall, as if shutting events off from itself from the very start. In front of the brick wall stands a small table: a bottle of milk on it. With his back to the spectators, a blond boy sits on his stool. Sheryl comes in from the left, rippling in her slowness like a nun possessed, and rigid as a seminarist preparing to commit the first sin of his priesthood. Sheryl's every step is aimed *for this* and *against this*. First she tenderly gives the child a drink, then replaces the empty bottle. How and what she performs is a rite rather than a sin, more precisely: the fulfilment, more burdensome and abstract than any duty, of the last phase of a sin. First of all she has to dress. She pulls her elbow-high black gloves onto both arms, hands. Then she has to take in her hand and open the razor laid ready on the table, and with it she then cuts the child's throat in a split second, while with her free left hand she has already covered him over.

In a few moments the sheet is blood-soaked from head to toe, but before Sheryl can go off she still has to close the razor and put it back. From then on one can sense that she has become weightless and steps unsteppingly, that all she would like to do is to sleep, that she is already asleep, but before that she still has to get out. And she does make an attempt to do so when a black boy, the same age as the one she has killed, blocks her way. Like vomit a howl breaks out from the boy. Sheryl claps her gloved hand over the boy's mouth, producing silence. Sheryl takes back her hand, when a deaf-mute's characteristic howl breaks out again from the boy, a sound such as never has heard any kind of sound. Sheryl claps his mouth up for the second time until the child's body calms under her hand, and now they can stand facing each other soundlessly. Sheryl turns and steps backwards to the middle of the brick wall. The little boy rhythmically in her tracks. Sheryl stops, and the child too behind her. Sheryl turns and starts walking straight at the stone wall. Up runs the brick wall, and the house lights go out. On a snow-white piano a black girl plays Chopin. The moon-lit park full of unrecognizable invited guests. Sheryl and the boy in her tracks, as I've earlier described, enter the garden and disappear from our view.

The fourth act takes place *outside and inside*. Outside the cave and inside the cave. From inside the cave, pure light. Outside the cave Sheryl is sitting, perhaps, in the exterior darkness and the fur of animals shivering in heaps shines, somehow like the stacks of shaved hair in the huge hall of the Auschwitz museum. But these heaps separate from time to time, and then merge again, shivering. Maybe they claw, maybe they huddle for warmth and console each other. Probably the retching black boy and the slain white boy are here too, but they are unrecognizable, just like Sheryl perching in the background. Even if one of them crawls and moans right here in the foreground, till hundredweight bodies settle in a soft pile round him. With difficulty and in confusion, however, being swept and hindered by strange impulses, but in the end closely and completely.

Meanwhile the light inside the cave is at times paradisal, at times infernal, a purgatorial light at times, according to which the demeanour of the naked bodies unceasingly swirls and changes. From this point, when the decisive iron grille crashes down in the cave's entrance, it is impossible to tell who are locked in and what it shuts out. So with the angel appearing and taking up his post behind the vertical iron bars, we don't know whether he really is an angel. As if we were looking into the sun, so the face of this overheated creature melts and changes in our eyes from an archangel into a giant locust, and from locust to angel.

The fifth scene: *Supper at the Frog-King's*. This act was the closest to fairytale, the most seaweedy, if you like: the greenest, sheer green. The seaweed air itself croaked, as if the stage's depth was nothing but childhood confidence and the anxieties of late childhood.

With the anxieties of late childhood I'll begin. To the left the Frog-King, grown tall and fattened up, already sat in princely exactitude at the head of the table. He permitted the waiter, red-wigged Rosenkrantz, to help the emblazoned chair into place beneath him and to attach the phosphorescent napkin to his neck. No hurry at all! No hanging about! The three people, father, mother and their nubile daughter, can only lose by being late. Wordlessly and defeated at the outset, they take their seats at the table.

The wedding candles have been burning for minutes by this time; Rosenkrantz fills the glasses with ice-cold wine. First the frog's, then the grey mother's, next the surpassingly beautiful nubile girl's, and last the father's. After the feast fit for a wake, the reptile rattles his diamonds in his webbed hands and lays them out on the table. The father reaches out for them one by one, from a distance. He too rattles them, he too lays them out.

Mother and daughter take no part in the bargaining that goes on across the table-cloth.

A swing high above goes back and forth. A child is swinging on it, a boy, it could be any boy in the world. The child Robert Wilson just as much as you or me or the child Homer or the retching black boy, or the other one who was killed. From the swamp-depth of the reeds, servile peasants push forth an ox that runs on wheels. From high above, glittering in a rounded, crinkly way, some tin foil several yards in diameter descends. The wheeled animal eats up the sun that swings in front of its nose as if it were browsing grass.

The swing stops; the child buries his face in his hands. First the father and then the mother get up and leave the table. The ox brightens up, like the rising sun. The frog makes no approach to the girl, and the peasants push the ox back from pasture.

The sixth and final act was seemingly the weakest. Here Wilson drew all his characters together, and simply burnt them, like a piece of paper. But when the play ended with this, the actors didn't come down in front of the curtain for the tumult of applause. The curtain rose again as for another act, so that the many groups of actors could acknowledge the ovation. An odd "bow", this. Instead of saluting the spectators, Wilson preferred the resurrection and apotheosis of his characters. Everyone was on the set again, though now jumping about, tossing bananas and oranges into the air and raising the dust to the ceiling in their unbridled high spirits. This irregular bow and ecstatic "salutation" was intended however not for the audience but for the story, the finished act of play itself. Someone kept catching the falling fruit with acrobatic skill, another kept dropping and clumsily chasing after the oranges that had rolled away. There could even have been some hundred people onstage, and probably not just the blind man, the square-shouldered, silver-soaked old woman, the two old-German peasant girls but – now at last in their human form – the Frog-King, the animals shivering in heaps or the archangel disguised as a locust, too. And in the centre, of course, springing higher than anyone, Sheryl. Her face appeared now with the severity of a black seminarist, now with an enraptured young girl's set of teeth, as she kept snatching the tossed fruit far above the heads of the crowd.

CHAPTER NINE

Deafman Glance *as Sheryl Sutton and I saw it*

SHERYL SUTTON: Shall we do some "modelling"?

(For the first and only time I was frightened by Sheryl. While I was asleep she managed to slip in so noiselessly that her face was all at once above mine.)

— : Sheryl *(But first I sat up, so as to come to)*, I'm very tired.

SHERYL SUTTON: Show me your palm! Your left actually . . . As if it were insufficient, or just verged on your having reached manhood! The right, however, is definitely interesting, the only odd thing here is how such lines can be so faint, almost non-existent?

— : I'd like to go back once more, if not perhaps for the last time, to Wilson. But I wonder how valid the judgement of feverish and depressed people is? Because I'm feverish now and depressed, too. Interestingly, I used to think about this even in my adolescence. When I was ill with a fever I could only handle Tolstoy, Dickens and the big Brehm. Baudelaire for example, whom I absolutely adored, I was quite unable to think of.

The funniest thing of all, which after years I feel even more, is that *Deafman Glance*, though born in the course of protracted experimentation, is still not an experimental play. The way I find Beckett's plays for example so self-contained and worked out, like the plays of some twentieth-century Racine. What they open, they very strictly complete, even shut. They are closed like a clock's mechanism. Otherwise I'm no enemy of experimental theatre. But you know too that true experiment requires a closed test-tube, so that we learn how material behaves when constrained under artificial conditions, what kind of new changes and qualities it conveys about itself. Most experimental plays – unfortunately – are brewed in an open pot rather than an interrogation tube, and they only decompose the old, the normal, the impermanent without really forcing new words, new situations, new confessions from them.

When the art of the modern world fell under the influence of scientific thought, I'm afraid it lost its original self-sufficiency. What for the sciences resulted in endless control and fertile precision as a fruit of this, in art – paradoxically – sank sentence, word, text and form to beneath the level of the erstwhile "silence that cannot be dumbed" (unreplaceable even by the most perfect order and the most complete confusion of words, surpassing every kind of order and disintegration). Mostly it produced controversial performances, presence, chain reactions, instead of coalescing, burning together into a brand-new, unfathomable whole in the spirit of a real revolution or metamorphosis. Instead of leading to the stealthily acquired and envied precision of the sciences, the eternal control of words and sentences led to narcissism. You'll observe: *since that time* we've been able to talk about good stylistics, ridiculous as it would be to state of Homer or Shakespeare that they were good stylists. Instead of the stealthily acquired and envied precision of the sciences, and an oblivious precision at that, literature influenced by the continual self-control and self-justification of the natural sciences has changed to the very contrary, to being too stylish, as opposed to blind Homer, a "mirror-literature" winding its nightgown around itself. Of course here too there may be exceptions. Think of Weil, Gombrowicz. But mainly Dostoyevsky. In his rapture he really was writing in a blind way, with his back to the mirror. He was a bad stylist. His sentences landed where they fell. There was a place for them to land, and a place for them to fall.

SHERYL SUTTON: Wilson's play can easily be regarded as the recollection of surrealism, but a criticism of it at the same time, a transcendence of it too. That's why some surrealists hailed it so enthusiastically. They didn't realize that they were applauding and encoring the amen of their own memorial service.

In my own, probably simple-minded way, I see surrealism really as a product of an artificial world placed under artificial conditions. This is not how dreaming and the subconscious work. Depression doesn't, either, I can tell you. In surrealism, as in a man-made intellectual planet, the weight of things is lost first. Then proportions. After that, daubing and fitting the concrete facts together like a montage is child's play now. What's more: the more scrupulously you depict the elements in their weightless state, emptied, deprived of their proportions, the easier the "jigsaw" with them.

— : But in what way could Wilson transcend surrealism?

SHERYL SUTTON: In that first he heated up the open or latent elements of montage, and then smelted them into a single ball. I can't find a better word than the smelted ball. In the depth of every work of art *it* rolls visibly or invisibly, rumbling, but mostly in silence. Though Wilson also subjected to examination – rather like your New York-researcher from Székesfehérvár, Mr Környei's snow-white factory building – the world, man, yes, pure substance. He loosened the reins even more than the surrealists, but then gradually drew down and descended into that stable, that smelting-furnace which we know as crime and punishment, or the press of the unrepeatable and concrete, of their reality staring us steadily in the face throughout a lifetime, where Shakespeare and the Greeks so unerringly hit the mark. It's the test-tube, that is to say, which is perfectly closed, like depression, but blazes up to the sky at the same time, like a temperature over 104°. The unrepeatable and single common place of experiment and mastery.

— : We've already talked about what is beyond boredom, but in relation to Wilson we could just as well be speaking of the silence beyond silence and the beauty beyond beauty. With him, dumbness is speech that cannot be dumbed, and what is beyond beauty – whether beautiful or ugly – has a swan's neck too, *everything is beautiful again*, like blind Homer's "rosy fingers" with which his imagination felt out the dawning sea.

Wilson has discovered what fever-sufferers can see and the depressed can bear. Blind Homer, so to say, has put a compress on the gory facts.

On this side of the demarcation line we know a lot: the asceticism of ugliness, the "literary" apparently being shed by the hyper-literary, the over-drawn poster's shock, the montage of emptied reality, the acrophobic, unceasing somersault of absurdities. Following the example of the old classics, Wilson had the strength to outlast and to transcend boredom, ugliness taken for a walk in the limelight and silence devalued to backchat. "No hurry at all!" the napkinned Frog-King could declare in his reptilian calmness. Later – after the dreaded demarcation line – we may or we may not,. but without patience certainly will not, reach that silence beyond boredom which is the single place of beauty beyond beauty and ugliness, and of speech beyond words. In this sense *Deafman Glance* is this century's only beautiful, sea-calm work of art free from all acrophobia. An avant-garde work of the sort which in a Dostoyevskyan sense could even belong to the arrière-garde. Modern in the way of Dostoyevsky's work *The Devils*, which the young of his age condemned because they pronounced it old-fashioned. What does it matter! There is a kind of arrière-garde without which no modern artist exists, at best an actualist, like Zola, a typical dupe of the moment.

The true modern was Dostoyevsky, and at the same time – of course – the exile of the moment, too. I should say: such a village idiot of a genius as alone is able to show what nobody can see, even if it stares them in the face, and what alone is real and burdened with developments. The Easter sacred picture afore-mentioned, grubby from being kissed, doesn't – after all – mean tradition for us, but a ramshackle object, like the empty spectacles-frames accumulated in the Auschwitz museum.

Well: what is truly beautiful with Wilson, beautiful *again*, beyond boredom and dumb, is ghostly in my eyes as the Auschwitz museum can be, when because of intense cold it has no visitors. It goes on dawning unchangingly with its hair-piles and spectacles-heaps and its rags spread out on the ground of stone-floored rooms. *Deafman Glance* you don't have to see. *Deafman Glance* simply exists, just as even on a mass of unpublished stars more majestic changes than earthly dawns must take place regularly on the dot. The play – in this sense – is really a world-model. That is to say, the kind of ball that rolls even if it's not "performed". The way truth exists and has an influence even in those cities where nobody tells the truth and where all acts are hypocrisy.

"I feel there lived a golden bough in my head which will disappear on my death without leaving a trace. What does it matter! The mine is inexhaustible!"

SHERYL SUTTON: Simone Weil.

— : Yes, but at the same time it has become my own "aesthetic". In my view man, in spite of all appearances, is a citizen not only of the earth but of the universe too. He loses not one hair unremarked, though all that's his is in a prodigal estate and in vain. Wilson's play also influences everything and everyone, although it has no script. So the knocks and scratches on the Auschwitz mess-tins are unceasingly *writing*, lit-up or in the silence of the night. I would drop dead if just a single night star passed away and those knocks, dents and scratches meant no more than duplicated conveyings, if they didn't tally with that mine which – in Simone Weil's word – is inexhaustible.

SHERYL SUTTON: Great works accordingly are *written* not in line with the earth's, more precisely not only the earth's, but the universe's *ars poetica*?

— : Yes, but in a provincial way sometimes, like folk-baroque.

SHERYL SUTTON: Tell me honestly, don't you occasionally

regret that you didn't pursue the labyrinth of your left palm?

— : That's a good question. Lost in the perishable, perhaps I could see more precisely wherever I've got to, and fastened in the electric chair . . .

SHERYL SUTTON: We all live strapped into the electric chair. When I'm acting, my only prompter is the perishableness written in your left palm. That's the truth. The fact that in the meantime I move and live is a film-thin appearance. I was in the right place for me when I was sitting on my throne. And *that's why* I broke into a sweat when I had to stand up. Wilson is really a master in this. That's why he managed to mould the montage into a ball, and roll it away on its orbit. Because the equivalent of our freedom *here and now* can only be the recognition, acceptance and unconditional love of that helpless rolling. That is: only this way can we become from earthly mortals something we all know about but which we forget and deny every moment. Our jumping about and unbridled high spirits were intended for that: in the performance of a bitter struggle, the gradually recognized citizenry and homeland of which our solar system is but an illusory border country.

CHAPTER TEN

On dialogue – Mass and acting – Actors and audience – At night in New York

— : And dialogue?

SHERYL SUTTON: Dialogue! I knew you were going to ask that. Well, what I think about it is what you think too. The trouble didn't start with it, of course, the trouble just came to a head with it. Where then, and when? I couldn't point to it. It came, like subterranean water. At the point, I think, when we left baroque theatre behind, and were looking for something more raw, more naturalistic instead of it. Nobody noticed that this was already an omen of the catastrophe at the gates. Perhaps this was only suspected by poets. On the eve of naturalism Baudelaire attempted to establish a cult of the unnatural. But from that period, how far have we gone! Now, it seems – from the trees of Eden! In our days, poets talk first about lack of world, and now even about loss of presence. And slowly, not only poets but children growing up, even if they keep silent about it, if they drag it around and keep obstinately silent about it. The subterranean water didn't come in through the gates but all at once flooded the city, and stage and audience, of course, as well as streets and homes. But about that, later. Let's talk now simply about why the dialogue of the naturalistic theatre has become a lie, from one hour to the next.

— : Because, we believed at first, spontaneous and everyday dialogue is impossible to repeat through fifty to a hundred evenings. The actors' word-mimicking art can be the most illusory product of "the natural", their *attention is incapable* of the continuous job of imitation. In dialogue, and primarily in dialogue, they pay more and more attention to themselves from performance to performance, expecting at best their cues from the other. Forced into pairs like this, they gesticulate more and more solitarily, and finally have no more presence.

SHERYL SUTTON: That's why Wilson chose silence. Others again, as a solution to the impossible situation, put words and answers impossible from the start into their heroes' and heroines' mouths. Or they stripped the action and diction to the so philosophical that it always mows into *something* with its conceptual force. That way even if they weren't creating a brand-new theatre, at least they weren't telling lies. Wilson's silence – yes, while acting I always felt that at last we could really talk . . . Then on the way home, catching sight of a young boy standing around and keeping obstinately silent in front of the game-table, the question burst up from me with irresistible power: is it finally impossible again to find the poetic word which in its essence has always been silence? Dialogue, which is silence, word, the weekday and the ritual of itself at the same time, not only breaking but also deepening the reserve of youngsters? Deepening their silence, so as to bring them to speak, bring them back to "dialogue"? And the stage to some such speech and dialogue that in tempo resembles an aeroplane's movement? We feel that we're standing, though we're speeding along and getting there! We *find our way home*, which obstinate silence by itself will never be able to, neither at home, nor shut in its room, nor in the street, nor beside the game-table.

— : In saying this you unwittingly drew my attention to what you mentioned about the Catholic mass. Have you noticed that there's no difference between a silent and a sung mass? Why is that, how can it be possible?

SHERYL SUTTON: Yes, I've already thought about that, in fact when I had once left something on stage and had to go back for it. Then I stopped for a minute, as in the middle of a blacked-out, shorted amusement arcade. And then – with my eyes shut – I had an idea. What would happen if we began to talk again on stage, in real monologues and real dialogues? But not as up to now, rather – at least to start with – openly and avowedly *talking to ourselves*? The way priest and ministrants, priest and congregation mutter, talk, the way priest and choir sing to themselves, and yet aren't alone, yet are somehow together. If we too talked like this – I went on with pitiful inspiration – we would at first probably remain alone on the stage for a very long time to come. But who knows, perhaps one day in an unexpected moment we could manage to put a stop to what keeps the city occupied? To reconquer the word and presence?

— : The city of New York . . . Fascinating at nightfall. I had dinner at a place where the damask table-cloths reached the floor, and between the pedestalled glass bowls a candle shone. The carpet soft and thick; the old black servant's hair silver-white. As if in *Uncle Tom's Cabin* I sat at the plantation-owner's table waiting for when the children would run in to say good-night, to sit on laps for a while and to linger until the black nannies standing about at the rail and the English governesses who accompany them pack the children off to bed in the bedroom upstairs.

After this, an hour and a half's lecture and debate on structuralism, then a glass of wine at the assistant professor's apartment – she was of Belgian origin. Everybody is ready to leave, we only stay for the sake of an elderly lady who's waiting for her husband. The man arrives late, in a long cape and velvet hat. We take our leave at once and are on our way.

The skyscrapers now live further away than seals and flamingoes. What's down is all that counts. The young woman walking a bloodhound and the figure loitering a hundred yards away from her. From the car we're already shooting glances at the skyscrapers too. Leaving Broadway, we speed along on the edge of Harlem. Shop-windows, fleeting shadows, youths. Shop-windows which, even standing beside one another, are lonelier than highway petrol-stations.

SHERYL SUTTON: Were you all frightened?

— : We were happy when we got back to New Haven. I was

particularly happy, even. I waited up until the whole house had fallen sound asleep and then went down to the carpeted kitchen. The Siberian dog had already joined me on the wooden stairs, he almost lent me a hand in making coffee.

You know, by then I had got perfectly used to one of his eyes being blue and the other brown. But what's this look he's giving me? What kind of abyss does he and does he not jump, does he and does he not bridge?

You see, theatre should jump anew the space that gapes between spectacle and onlooker, subject and object. In such a way, with such strength, like . . . Or rather, the way this dog does! With his glance, he uncovered the entire tragic side of our existence. The fact that we are one, and the fact that we are not one. The fact that we live torn into smaller and smaller islands, and finally perhaps live not on islands even, but in the panic of loneliness hanging on at the top of a column, nailed onto a pin-point. In a word: illuminated and forgotten.

Yes, this Siberian dog is *quite sure* to have been standing before me. And the way he was present, no one could look more deeply, more persistently into my eyes.

SHERYL SUTTON: Did you close your eyes, at least?

— : I didn't have to close them.

SHERYL SUTTON: All right, then.

(That afternoon Sheryl was wearing the same ground-length dress in which she appeared in Deafman Glance.*)*

— : What are you thinking about *now*, Sheryl?

SHERYL SUTTON: New York. Finally I just wanted to sleep, night and day. But fear has no eyelids.

— : Yes, nor does confidence.

SHERYL SUTTON: That's why I said *all right*.

CHAPTER ELEVEN

The reality of the stage – When someone gives a slight cough in the auditorium – How Wilsonian theatre annexed and excluded the incidental – Difficulties of the last act

— : I'm cold. In the other room, there's another blanket in the cupboard. Thank you.

The collapse of dialogue – naturally – was only the most conspicuous consequence of the total collapse of the pyramid's top, of the pyramid. Fundamentally the reality of the stage ceased to exist, and the audience's eyes were burned out. Today a slight cough in the auditorium is enough for the stage to be annihilated. A slight cough is a thousand times more valid than the most apposite sentences and gestures in the limelight.

SHERYL SUTTON: Wilson was quite aware of this, too. In his playing he has simultaneously built in the perfect and the imperfect, the incidental and the indisputable, the disabled person and the athlete. What fell to me was star-movement, the security of wild animals, but at the same time the stage was filled around me with the stumbling of people hired off the street in their suits with worn-out elbows, their slovenly hip-pockets, civilian movement. Anyone could have coughed now. The scenery could even have crashed. Neither the bed nor the surface of the play's flow could have been further disturbed.

Orthodox Easter? God's stable? Well, yes. Coming and going and the closed iconostasis. Wilson succeeded in completing the perfect with the incidental, and vice versa. The perfect and the imperfect were waiting with open arms for whatever at all could happen in the city. All five acts, in fact, were the staging of slight coughs from the auditorium.

— : The ending alone didn't work.

SHERYL SUTTON: I'm afraid you're right.

— : The main temptation and failing of the last act is that it becomes a summary.

SHERYL SUTTON: A sunset.

— : It's when schoolboys rule a line and add up the columns of numbers.

SHERYL SUTTON: But what else can you do?

— : What you did.

SHERYL SUTTON: Which was?

— : Probably it was your idea. I'm hinting at your mother's protestant meetings. Nobody came out in front of the curtain. The curtain was forced to rise, even if perspiringly, sweatily. And there was everyone again on stage, yet now no longer being summed up but in unrestrained order, as we live, or rather as we would like to find salvation. One wolf, one lamb; one black, one white.

SHERYL SUTTON: *(Squinting.)* You're right, but why did the curtain have such difficulty in rising?

— : Sheryl, you're asking a question where one can only cease to exist or to act.

SHERYL SUTTON: *(With a squinting smile.)* Meaning, you're hungry?

— : Sheryl, make a nice potato goulash.

SHERYL SUTTON: *(From the kitchen already.)* Your schoolboys are now adding up the columns of numbers. Strange: night falls at the same time in Paris and New York. Maybe because of the ocean? The sea is large enough to solve the difficulties of the ending, the adding-up. In my opinion we always have to begin everything from the beginning. But not at nightfall any more, but at night, in the pit. Everyone has to be hauled onto stage again. The children most of all.

— : Sheryl, I didn't thank you for nursing me until now.

SHERYL SUTTON: My hands are oniony.

— : *(After a long pause.)* The Siberian dog wasn't just looking at me, it's looking at me now.

SHERYL SUTTON: *(With sudden hilarity.)* I'd rather it helped me chop onions!

— : This dog is a better solution than the sea.

SHERYL SUTTON: A better solution for what?
— : For the last act.

CHAPTER TWELVE

Before Auschwitz, after Auschwitz – Simone Weil on beauty – Strange cohabitation

SHERYL SUTTON: I wanted to go to sleep, finally just to sleep night and day. But fear has no eyelds. I saw the trash-cans and the boys' fighting. Every corridor, staircase, gateway. Every bulb left burning. As the skyscrapers' heads nod off in the rain. The whole city in pieces and all at once.

— : According to Adorno, after Auschwitz it's impossible to write poems any more.

SHERYL SUTTON: That's the kind of saying of which the opposite is equally true, if not truer. Listen to this: "After Auschwitz, poetry is possible again." It's true, though, that Auschwitz cracked time. Since then it's been impossible for us not to distinguish what was before Auschwitz from what was and was yet to come after Auschwitz.

Today we have a better understanding of Proust's and Rilke's asceticism swelling beneath the artistic surface. Not self-torture but premonition was at work in them.

— : In modern times I know of two writers who prepared themselves in spirit and in their whole beings for what came to pass. The first is Franz Kafka, and the second Simone Weil.

SHERYL SUTTON: You said that from the war and from the camps we recovered the vocabulary of poverty and great literature together. Things like "I'm starving", "I'm cold", "I ask, and am not given", and of course also "I ask, and am given."

— : Yes, I see in this the Copernican turning-point. Naturally there were hasty reactions, and there still are today: misfortune is hard not only to bear but also to examine and to observe. And yet – in Simone Weil's words – there's no beauty of higher degree than the authentic description of misfortune.

SHERYL SUTTON: Every word is important in that sentence. But a Bach's exceptional strength is needed for it.

— : That's not absolutely certain. After the war we could witness almost year by year a phenomenon nearly fit for a biological riddle. Young people in large numbers became talented or at least receptive and sensitive, eccentric and silent. What happened? – we all wondered. I've even strung a theory together for personal use to explain this unusual apparition. Previously – I thought – only talented individuals had the power to destroy the world fossilized every so often from convention, then to build it up for themselves in its original freshness. Now this is a quite different case. Today before the very eyes of youth, and what's more the whole of youth, the world collapsed, like the tower of Babel or the walls of Jericho. As regards them, then, what comes to one's mind is not so much the individuals of genius but rather the situation of genius, into which all of them are forced, the weak and the strong, the talented and the untalented too. What will happen to them, what will become of them? Will their strength be sufficient to establish the world which *they* haven't destroyed? Or will their destiny be what used to be that of the half-talented, the broken-backed geniuses whose strength was equal only to half their task?

SHERYL SUTTON: It's raining again! And I didn't bring a coat. The world would need great silence. If it were up to me I would order all theatres, all printers and publishing houses to be closed down for ten years. Ten years at least, so that we could at last examine where we are, and where we're heading. Just imagine, one fine day we would wake up to find silence. No cinema, no theatre, only it's drizzling. Don't get me wrong, I absolutely respected and understood Sajna's post-Auschwitz theatre, and later Antonin Artaud and Grotowski, but especially Beckett's end-of-the-world tug-of-war. What I don't like, and particularly don't like on your continent, are the countless manifestos which shatter the essential silence of works. Remember that Beckett is of Irish origin; that Wilson came without a word, nor did he make any statement after his success; think of Sylvia Plath's schizophrenic prudishness; or take Francis Bacon as opposed to the surrealists, and you'll see at once what kind of keeping silent I'm hinting at.

— : This is probably true in rough outline, at least in the arts. Anglo-Saxons are protected by their instinctive complexity, individualism and tolerance; these make any kind of theoretical grouping – without which, however, there is no *school* in an intellectual sense – impossible for them. Because for manifestos, for their blessings and excommunications, two things are needed: the inclination to abstraction and the compulsive making absolute of one realization or another. The British, in their heart of hearts, are incapable of any such thing, they are too eccentric, and perhaps too prudish to trim their groves and woods into French gardens.

SHERYL SUTTON: In spite of this – for different reasons perhaps – we too would need silence.

— : You probably know this better than I do. There's no denying the fact, though, that more and more often – and nearly always by chance and clumsily – a silent young American emerges to astonish Europe with what he pieces together to perfection in New York or in countryside solitude during long, long years of great secrecy. In the past saints may have lived, and anarchists bent on death may have appeared like this. In a grey way, in silence with a briefcase under their arm. But in this briefcase there was real dynamite. Monks can still be recognized; saints can't, now. Just as -isms *must be recognized*, but masterpieces – even in the service of some -ism or other – are now very hard to, and it's only possible step by step.

SHERYL SUTTON: It's only you who think that these boys and girls don't know what they're doing. Yet it's you people who still don't know the unbearable pressure of noise and material. That freckled young man who sits on the tenth floor and from morning to night keeps on sticking together a never-seen puppet show, while at best having a snack or blowing his nose – he knows at least as much not only about material and noise, but about silence and the work-bench too, and in my opinion much more than the most laconic medieval peasants of the earth and the weekly market.

Your sin is that you only ever take notice of these young masters for this or that reason, especially if they come from other parts of the world. Our sin, however, is that we don't take any notice of them at all. For all we care they could stay in the country or upstairs for good. Well, that's why we need silence like a spring shower.

— : Are you going back to New York?

SHERYL SUTTON: Only to act. Even in Paris I'm afraid. Most of all I'd like to move to the country.

— : Aren't young people any consolation to you? Their reserve.

SHERYL SUTTON: That's true. In the world today there are masses of (I say this in inverted commas) "newborns" and masses of (this I'm not saying in inverted commas) survivors. Newborns who in a mysterious way know all that the survivors do, and survivors who in an uncanny way understand the speech of newborns and their reserve; soon they are paying attention to the newborns alone. But the world does not consist only of newborns and survivors! That, then, is why I long for the country, where the fact that a shopkeeper takes half an hour over weighing a pound of sugar for my basket loses me not a minute.

— : And the theatre?

SHERYL SUTTON: Thank God, I'm black, an American black, what's more. We all are over something. Over sin, deed . . . Whatever. We were born this way, in fact. Most of us are cheerful, but sombre too. Most teenagers loll against the wall of a house all day long, and once they stir, you wish they wouldn't. So your question, with that emphasis, makes no sense. For me at least, let's say. I became an actress too, no doubt, because with my ninety pounds I weighed several tons. And why, do you suppose? This is an act of God which all the same I wouldn't give up for anything. One day everybody will be sitting about like this. All of you will. You, too.

CHAPTER THIRTEEN

On loss of presence – The sat-out armchair – From theatre to kitchen – Horizontal and vertical; different kinds of experiment; the provocative theatre – Hölderlin's late poems

SHERYL SUTTON: What we were discussing about loss of presence is valid not only on the stage but for our whole lives. I wonder how much further it can be intensified? It's so hard for me to talk clearly about all this, even though it's clear as daylight. It is most striking in the case of box-office hits and failed experimental theatres. But let's stay with box-office plays, which we've previously also called mimicry-theatre. Let's suppose that the set, the costumes, the actors and the play are: the deceptive die-casts of mimicry, of "reality". Of course they imitate with this what from the outset doesn't imitate anything: the unrollable-up wonder of life. But let's go a step further. Why has nobody, nobody for decades noticed this, taking delight in it for hours as in a female impersonator's sketch? Probably because delusion and self-delusion are for a certain time more comfortable than the most sat-out armchair. With the right lie, generations can be stuck in it.

But all the same trouble is trouble, and it's getting worse, too. First a rare bird, then crowds, then finally actors, directors, dramaturgs and theatre managers have also noticed it. From then on, instead of the security of demi-gods, helplessness, disillusion and the theatre "business" began to roll what for a long, long time has been manners, costume, inconveniently transparent delusion, and the more it was made to spin, the more it became a top giving out slower and falser sounds.

From here it's more and more difficult for me to find the words. For lack of a better I would say: we have lost our presence. All at once, in fact, at home, in the street, on the staircase, on stage, in the auditorium, in bed and in the kitchen. We wanted at all costs to be present, yet it was just our presence that we lost, just the certainty, as the cramped grip loses what it grasps, jealousy what it spies on, as goggling eyes don't finally see what they are staring at. The real became *nothing*, and then the even-more-evil-than-nothing *as-if*, the as-if more tormenting than lack, even by rejecting and destroying which we cannot get back to certainty and presence.

— : This is rather as if the predicate had disappeared from our sentences. Help, Sheryl! Our life has become sentences in which attributes, adverbs, articles, nouns, singulars and plurals continue to have a place, even to multiply – only the predicate *does not happen*. It stands there but it is not present. As if our sentences – and of course our life too – had only a level expansion, a lowland, a horizontality without the vertical of predicates, the perpendicular of the here and now nailing them down, digging them in, making them have happened. Am I talking confusedly? This is how the world has become *as-if*. An imitation. A more and more empty and more and more miserable *as-if*. How far we are from lack! Nothing made us feel desperate, at least.

Perhaps it's simplest if I use a biblical image. When the angel chased us out of Paradise, not only were "our minds darkened and our will made weak", but our imagination also faded. Since then the world, even for our eyes and imagination, has not been a completed whole. For its reality the incessant work of our imagination is needed, not only the work of our minds and the sweat of our will but perhaps even more the eternal filling out and contribution of our imagination, so as to "get somehow from the facts to reality". And this is not the private business of poets and artists, their Sisyphean undertaking, but the universal drama of all people, of the human imagination. It is just this gaping lack that imitation misses. That's why the mimicry-stage could have become empty, and why the most deceived spectator, even if not in the theatre or immediately after the theatre, but now at home on the staircase or at the latest in the bathroom, as if he was standing not in front of the bath-tub, but now *only* in front of the bath-tub.

As-if rather than *nothing* has broken into our world, has become unbearable. But let's stay with theatre.

SHERYL SUTTON: We discovered the trouble late, but relatively quite early. I think of some "cornered" geniuses. One attempted with emblems and symbols to heat up the ephemeral, transformed into a pocket-watch. Another to make a self-contained poetic quality, a poetic poetry, out of what doesn't need just the poetic, if indeed it is ever poetry. The third could now afford to be more radical and resourceful: he "created" new formulae which however were trying to snatch, to *invent* from reality precisely the inimitable, after the childhood diseases of fantasy and the artifices of imitators too old, establishing again the future of *creative imagination*. The fourth, by rejecting almost all kinds of construction, flooded the stage with poetry's drily glowing sunspots and outbursts. The fifth – say – was Beckett. Even with bare hands he managed at once to bring the essence to stage, the end-of-the-world, matter-of-life-and-death tug-of-war. And finally there were some who found obsession a more effective spur than facts, and stayed close to plays of the past only in structure, striving to squeeze the most fire from it, as persistently as from a lemon.

I won't speak of Wilson's co-ordinated, many-sided breakthrough and my own daydreams. But it would be proper to spend a few words on aggressive theatre. Nobody has ever been convinced or helped home by hustling and jostling. Frightened, perhaps. I have, however, too often been afraid, so am content with the creative invention and bloodless ritual of reality.

— : What would happen, you said, if Wilson's figures started to speak? You said that at first they would probably just talk to themselves for a long time. This, though, brings me back, I think, to one of Heidegger's observations on the elderly

Hölderlin. That these poems are not the usual lyric visions and manifestations, but *discussions. Discussions* of his own tragic life. Don't you think that on stage too we should mutter, talk to ourselves in this way, carry on a *discussion* with everything and everybody, with our partner and with ourselves at the same time? Also on the subject of what we're talking about, but even more what we're not, and what we can't?

CHAPTER FOURTEEN

On "vertical theatre" again – Can theatre be a way of life? – Certainty and the end of the century

SHERYL SUTTON: Where do you place the absurd theatre?

— : In yesterday's horizontal, lowland theatre you found everything as in a house built on sand, only it had no cellar. To the point of delusion it *resembled*, except that it *hadn't happened*. The spectators, though, were more and more lost in the fever of making continual comparisons. Like the play, they weren't present, either. Because where did the play take place? *Here and now* on the stage, or *there and then*, which the play wishes to resemble and, equally, to be about? Everyone's eyes were on the actors, while their attention kept turning back and forth. Real trouble, though, came about – and maybe at the same time, maybe much earlier than in the theatre – when "everyday reality" began to lose one after another its predicates, presence, and moved, with at least one foot, first into nothing, then into a sort of indefinable *as-if*. From then on, theatre and "reality" alike have changed into a horizontal lowland, a lowland abounding in adjectives, nouns and adverbial phrases, into a house built on sand, without the cellar of the predicate, its vertical, its *here and now*.

The absurd theatre – to answer your question, in my own way of course – was perhaps nothing but the reconquest of the lost predicate. In the absurd, what is happening happens here and now, happens indeed, and it's no use our turning back and forth, there is nothing worth comparing it with. The only trouble is that the absurd theatre, given that it happens, essentially has already happened, has finished too.

The horizontal theatre is made to "steal" its collection of predicates, but the absurd theatre its attributes and adverbs, so that they could hold the stage for half an hour or an hour at least. Would both of them essentially suffer from the same thirst for air?

SHERYL SUTTON: I'm afraid so. Even if for my part I prefer the mere predicate's thirst for air to the gasping of attributes and nouns leading illusory lives. It's true though that – beyond the fact that it happens here and now, without any compulsion to keep comparing – any other "messages" of the absurd play remain below its own standard. One resembles a suicide: a moment is enough for it, but that moment actually comes about, here and nowhere else. The other, yesterday's theatre, is the kind of social event in which despite nice ankles and cunning machinations nothing on earth happens or can happen.

— : It's no accident that while renewing the theatre, Wilson was looking for a new way of life.

SHERYL SUTTON: In my opinion, too: we should rather speak not so much of a new theatre as of a new way of life. But we are still a long way from this, even if we've tried out all kinds of things. I'm not thinking here of the usual communes; much more of the manners of bearing, nods, stops and touchings, uncommittable anywhere else. We were wafting about in the darkness for hours – and were joking around, and got hurt, met and parted, absolutely as we pleased. Incredible how many innocent gestures we can't make in our lives even towards the most beloved beings! Even alone in our room, even in the deserted street, in sexuality, on the staircase, or in the elevator! Forever discouraged wild animals, by virtue of rehearsals we have committed a few unusual ones out of the millions. The nicest was when I was holding a little girl's face between my hands first for a moment, then for a minute, then for the whole rehearsal. Since then I'd like to hold it between my hands for a lifetime. Two kinds of human warmth have incredible words, far beyond the words that are known. If this dialogue could only begin to speak! But since I'm a child of the end of the century, what I say is, let's leave hidden what has so far been hidden as well! The world and me: two things. Let's shake hands on that! I can surpass my roles up to now, I can make sure and produce evidence of this or that . . . All the same! It's desperate.

Wilson applauded, placed the stuffed raven to my left, and made me sit down. In half an hour I stood up, and broke out into a sweat.

Two o'clock . . . Kick me out! By tomorrow you'll be ill again.

— : Sweet Sheryl, don't cry.

CHAPTER FIFTEEN

Motionless commitment – Motionless drama – Half asleep

(Sheryl stayed with me that night. I could hardly calm her down. She made a bed on the floor for herself and went to bed in her clothes and shoes, which I found particularly charming. Our eyes were still open for a long time in the dark.)

SHERYL SUTTON: Did I tell you about the girl in New Orleans? She had been saving up for weeks, stuffed her snack-money into a handkerchief so that she could go to the swimming pool in the city park. It was a beautiful swimming pool, fenced in by wire netting, with a sloping lawn at the edge.

— : *(I no longer know why I instinctively wanted to draw Sheryl's attention away.)* Do you know why you began to sweat when you stood up in the first scene? Because you really stood up. My favourite thought is that art is *engagement immobile*, motionless commitment, and real drama is (I read this later in Weil's "exercise books") *drame immobile*, motionless drama. The kind of movement, action that reminds one most of the stars' changing of places. Movement and motionlessness, that is, at the same time. But why? Because with the power of quality, it must penetrate into what in reality has irreversibly and definitively happened very long ago. It's finished, it's been done, it has come about. Every great work penetrates into where it can do no more. And still: it comes over, just as in once bloody and final events, Shakespeare and Sophocles carried out the first pure action, the way the past tense is busy with what is practically unchangeable, unsolvable moreover.

SHERYL SUTTON: The way Homer put a compress on the gory facts?

— : The comings and goings of the characters in masterpieces are only appearances. The play stands motionlessly in the palm of the past, or to be precise of quality. To be even more precise: into the finished and unredeemable, for the first time intrudes the real action. It is nothing but the intervention of the understanding quality, devotion, maturity and genius (speaking of theatre): poetry's intervention, without changing the facts at all. Everything can be enacted again though it is irreproducible, everything can be redeemed though unredeemable, is retrievable though irretrievable, and brand-new though it is definitively finished.

SHERYL SUTTON: Is this what you call motionless commitment?

— : I would say rather, I'm making an effort to stammer out what I think about it. The artist – and maybe no other soul – not only trots along after the earth's daily bread, but is a citizen of the universe too. But that's "motionless", like – in miniature – a fixed star; stronger and more powerful than everything, its restraint at the same time – apparently – does not make one feel under any obligation.

I've often wondered why good utopian novels are so rare. Well, just because the real medium of poetry, if it is poetry indeed, is the irretrievable. The future is too easy, too rare, not resistant enough for it. It is insufficient for the actual trial of strength, it's not able to act *purely* in it, at best it's daydreaming about it, or in fact, even at the cost of lies, escapes into it, with delusion or self-deception. For the artistic action, though, which at least is always motionless on its axis, like the posture of the thinking man: the unabsolvable and unsolvable past is not at all identical with the true or false treasury of reflections. Inexpressibly more than the lesson. That too. But first of all, the chosen ground of its "action". The call of closed and finished facts is always the strongest. Otherwise it would sense that even the brightest future is an amoral desert, with its cemeteries of left-behind, finished, unsolvable and irretrievable facts, cemeteries longing for *reality*, with the never ceasing call. That's why Leonardo could say that anyone who doesn't look around enough is wasting his whole time.

And when you stood up, it had such a tremendous strength, since we felt that your standing up had not really happened, because you had stood up.

SHERYL SUTTON: And motionless drama?

— : Well, yes; the other, the visible side of the same coin. Apparently most drama is action, depiction of one kind or another of what the playwright has "invented", or simply examined for one reason or another. In reality, though, it is motionless or even, rather, anti-motion, anti-action if for no other reason than its uniformity of standard. As every single part of a good sculpture says the same thing, and is eventually not harmonious: it is *one*. Unharmed even in ruins, and even mutilated, a whole. Every real drama stands, like the sun or a significant sentence. First perhaps it only slows down, but actually from beginning to end – despite all motion, all changing of places and actions, all appearances and all sights – it stands, and like a good deed has no time. The slowed-down movement of Wilson's theatre has made this truth even more obvious, for example, in my youth I wrote of "decay slowed-down to happiness".

Another question again, why in our age the literal can less and less be poetry, and why our attention turns to a greater degree towards rituals. That is, a ritual, even if the priest is unbelieving and the congregation is half asleep, through the strength of its truth is always capable of action in the drama which it would be unable to recall by means of any nail or vinegar. But we've already spoken of this, if I remember rightly.

Motionless drama (the "drame immobile") for me does not mean that it's perfectly motionless, like Prometheus on the rock, Jesus on the cross or a catatonic schizophrenic in the final stage of his illness. It's not by chance, though, that, at the peak of his tragedy, each person *turns to stone*. No. The "drame immobile" means the kind of motionlessness, rather of time beyond time which we feel, or don't feel, while listening to a piece of music. Of course it would be possible to write motionless plays in a literal sense, as generally speaking the tragedies of Aeschylus were. This depends on the capacity in which the artist is writing on paper. As a citizen just of earth, or just of the universe, or of both at once. Bach – even if on the same level of "quality" – was undoubtedly working as a citizen of the universe in composing his Mass in B minor, but as one of the universe and the earth, both at once, when writing his two Passions.

SHERYL SUTTON: The water of the pool was blue; I had already admired it through the wire netting. I got my money ready in my palm well in advance, from the handkerchief unknotted with my teeth. It was a bit more than the entrance fee, but I was still afraid that it wouldn't be enough. And of paying it all in small change. The ticket – I can still see it exactly now – was strikingly long, marked with a red stripe in the middle. At the entrance the bigger half of the ticket was torn off.

In the cabin I hung everything up on the same nail. Hanging on the wall there was also a small mirror, but I didn't look in it, only while I stuck the ticket behind it. I hesitated for minutes over whether to leave my shoes on, but then I took them off after all and went out barefoot. Nobody at home knew where I was. Hot July wind gently blowing away. I locked the cabin door and took the key with me in my hand.

— : Sheryl, why are you telling this story?

SHERYL SUTTON: As an example of when something important happens, which doesn't really happen.

Key in hand, I was heading straight for the pool when it hit me that I couldn't swim. What if they find that out? In the whole swimming pool I alone was black, and a girl under the shower who in turn was so white that I've never seen such white. And not just her skin, her hair was white too, whiter and whiter as it soaked, squeezed and pressed on her head under the water-jet. She didn't move, didn't turn this way and that, or close her eyes like the others. She let the water flow into her eyes.

I went back to the cabin, put on my clothes and went home.

— : Is that all?

SHERYL SUTTON: Everything that's a whole is like that.

— : If I sometimes keep my eyes open when I ought to close them, when others close them . . .

SHERYL SUTTON: This girl's eyes were red, and not because of the water.

— : It's time we went to sleep.

SHERYL SUTTON: We must keep our eyes open whenever and as long as possible.

— : But not long ago you were talking about confidence and fear . . .

SHERYL SUTTON: I'm half asleep already. We always have to wait until our eyes close by themselves.

— : Mustn't we close our eyes to anything?

SHERYL SUTTON: Motionless drama is perhaps true. But what I said about wholeness, that surely is.

— : Are you asleep yet, Sheryl?

SHERYL SUTTON: When I pulled the ticket out from under the mirror, I looked in it properly for the first time. I put my shoes on last of all. While I was lacing them, I sensed that I was helping the holes with the repeatedly licked shoe-laces. I was burning with guilt for having wasted my snack-money.

(When Sheryl left in the morning, I was still asleep. She had left a note on the table: "I'll come at mid-day, the usual time, you could sit by the window for an hour or two if you don't have a temperature.")

CHAPTER SIXTEEN

Dostoyevsky – Sheryl asks and answers – Various knockings

SHERYL SUTTON: If you were to stage Dostoyevsky's *Demons* now, would you dare change anything in his text?

— : I think I would. Out of sheer fidelity.

SHERYL SUTTON: And which character are you thinking of?

— : The one who theorizes about anarchy and the one who always wants to commit suicide. I would turn the two of them into one.

SHERYL SUTTON: Go on.

— : I'd keep the small town. The period costume and the saloon. But the theoretician would not hold forth standing in front of the table, but from the wardrobe. "Ladies and gentlemen! I'd like to acquaint you with my invention. The contraption is extremely cheap, it costs nearly nothing. A box, two plugs and a cord are what's needed. It works for one single minute a year, but in this one minute it's capable of manic depression, schizophrenia and once possibly even of suicide." Here the door would burst open and the wardrobe-dweller would fall to his knees in front of Stavrogin.

SHERYL SUTTON: That's as far as your insertion would go?

— : I don't know. Perhaps Stavrogin could say something new – just a couple of sentences. A couple of new sentences after a hundred years.

SHERYL SUTTON: Before going on with his old text, in Stavrogin's place I . . .

— : You'd ask . . .

SHERYL SUTTON: Yes, I'd ask under what circumstances this invention works? Whether the scene is, say, a wardrobe, or a sheep-walk . . . Then I would go away just the same, and in a few years' time hang myself just like Stavrogin.

In my opinion Dostoyevsky would really have liked to get to

know two kinds of people: the saint and the suicide. He was never really interested in what lay in between. Neither promising inventors, nor plugs and boxes with suicidal tendencies.

Who a suicide is, I can't tell. But who a saint is, at least for a moment? – I'd hazard a guess. A saint, for instance, is a murderer in hiding when his deed is being discovered and he's being nabbed. At this moment in everybody's eyes, and first of all to himself, he is *only* a murderer. Which is nonsense. At this moment the whole universe is on his side, and on its knees. In a world: helpless.

The suicide, that's different. The suicide is murderer and victim at once. He is the one who killed, and he too the one who is killed. We should sniff our way along two completely different tracks at once to see what and where he is. But this is hopeless and unnecessary, too. A glance is enough to tell you that he's the same kind of dead as others. And still unplaceable. The suicide is the repository of a secret even greater than death.

— : Maybe that of death as an end in itself?

SHERYL SUTTON: Someone should write a play which consisted only of questions. Or one in which there would only be knocking. In the first act it would be all small children knocking, in the second all very old folk. In the third act the scene would be empty, and now the closed doors would be hammered on from inside.

CHAPTER SEVENTEEN

On folk art – Knocks and scratches – The school of attention – My story with the Romanian lance-corporal – Parable of beauty

SHERYL SUTTON: A dazzling village idiot kept standing in the rain for hours. And then recounted what made him stop. This is how folk art was born. No one took the young man's words seriously, but no one could drive them from their minds. Memory was his proof-reader, his printer, his publisher. Meanwhile one or another person's whim or dullness made serious errors in it, which were corrected by yet other people's memories and ingenuity. This is how the non-recurring has gradually become universal, and the knocks and scratches that it took have become in the end just as true, organic and intimate or perhaps even more serious than what has been worn out, dented, forgotten and preserved.

— : The nicest is what you said about the knocks and scratches. Even at night and unread, these are writing. The mess-tins and the piles of spectacles, just as much as the misery, beauty and near-sty devotion of folk art, keep on writing at night, even in cold of twenty degrees below zero. The *common work* of geniuses and single-minded peasants, the way the inhabitants of Noah's Ark thronged as one on top of danger, when water got closer than crying, closer than the eyes of the fish.

From this Noah-community we mustn't manufacture any kind of ideology. Simone Weil has expressed it sharply. I quote from memory. "How can one love one's homeland? Our homeland can be legitimately loved only by way of the Greeks, by way of folksong and the gospel's history of suffering, only, that is, with sympathy." If we don't understand and we miss this *tone*, we become a curse and are lost. Instead of folksong's (and folk art's) truth and common, flood-surviving bark, we get entangled in the destructive and self-devouring bickerings of our own rightness. We are deservedly lost.

To avoid this we need the unconditional love of truth – and not of our own rightness. First of all, trained attention. The task of schools – far beyond the communication of knowledge – is the education of attention.

Simone Weil has a wonderful example for this. The true unfortunate does not let hands be laid on him, he disguises his misfortune to the world, but first of all to himself, like cancer patients. Charity towards them is atrocity, blunder. No wonder then, if charity makes them even more bitter, reserved, spiteful and hostile. It is only a trained attention, a perfect diagnosis which they can't resist.

What happened in the good Samaritan's case? An unfortunate was lying covered in blood at the edge of a ditch. Somebody came by, then another, but their attention wasn't trained. Then the third to come was the Samaritan, whose attention was trained. One glance was enough for him to size up the situation of the man lying at the side of the ditch, on the point of giving himself up. And because the Samaritan's attention and recognition was precise, he could no longer not take action. He acted automatically. And the unfortunate, who otherwise revolted against any kind of help and would have thrashed about cursing, could not resist precise help, just as the Samaritan couldn't not act, not take on his back and carry the dying man home. Then – writes Weil – both of them were absolutely pure water. Perfectly one. Love itself loved by them and in them, as even man is unable to love himself, although this is nearly every person's most stubborn and most impossible demand.

For folk art, it was exactly the above-described attention that from time to time gave accommodation, thread, loom, voice and clay. That in the meantime others dented it, shut it out, damaged and forgot it? That the masters were not themselves those who bore the unbearable the most beautifully? What does it matter! What does it matter in such art, where in possession of truth and beauty the scribe is just as defenceless and nameless as the illiterate or the industrious peasant who, growing old, leaves his house to the young.

Great works *write* even in darkness. Terror overcomes me if I think of the fact that one day perhaps I too will write something down, which later gets to the rubbish-dump like confiscated dresses, and remains like a scrawl that must go on and on writing.

The case of the good Samaritan happened once to me. I was a raw recruit and a Romanian lance-corporal picked on me at first sight. He was cruel like a fanatic. One night he knocked me awake to get some water for his flask. Half asleep, I was fumbling my way out to the huge barrel, but instead of turning it on, I pulled the tap and the plug out together.

The barracks door burst open and was filled. The corporal lowered his voice significantly. "What am I supposed to do with you, man? I'll give you ten minutes. In this time, sir, you will go down to the village, bring two horses, harness them, take the barrel down and fill it. Et cetera." I threw myself to the straw and just cried and cried. Then somebody touched me, as never before in my life. It was the Romanian. "Don't cry. I talked to the corporal, we'll bring up six buckets of water, that'll be enough for the night."

I stood up.

The Romanian: "Get your torch out of your case." How did he know that I had a torch? Are hatred and love omniscient?

He didn't let me fill and lug the buckets. I didn't protest. Three times we turned uphill, downhill. I just shone the light and let him haul, meanwhile I was blazing.

A friend of mine once said that about reality we have, at best, legends. He preferred the natural sciences. Simone Weil preferred a peculiar Christian "legend". The world – she professed – is not so much creation as God's fruit of renunciation. The solar eclipse of completeness.

God in himself is more than God and all his creatures together. The world was born in the madness of love, but it was indeed born, which is most apparent in pure material, that is on the lowest level. God and material since the beginning of genesis have been obeying each other unconditionally. Without this mutual obedience, material would only be an unsympathetic mill-wheel. But it grows beautiful from mutual obedience. The best example is the sea. If the sea were a merciful liquid, it would perhaps be better for us, but it might be less beautiful.

You accept, I suppose, the emphatic correlations of the cohabitation of beauty, mutual obedience, goodness and merciless mechanism in Simone Weil's "mythology". Finally, I recall from memory one of her parables about artistic beauty.

Beauty is a labyrinth. Many start in it, but get tired halfway. Some however are strong enough and reach the maze's centre. There God waits for them, gobbles them up and spews them out. Then they come out of the labyrinth, stand at the entrance and gently urge passers-by inward.

(Sheryl was unusually cheerful today. Here, though, she grew gloomy. And then she became almost sarcastic.)

SHERYL SUTTON: Laugh me down! When you were talking about the waiting of the Siberian dog, the little girl taking a shower, who was never waiting for anybody, came to my mind – for the first time in years. If there is salvation, it will be like that. The girl with white hair will always come after me, will already be following me on the wooden stairs, even at night, to lend me a hand in making coffee. One of her eyes is blue, the other brown. But both are red. Who is it?

— : You ask the right questions.

SHERYL SUTTON: In your place I would have said: "Sheryl, your shoe-laces lace the right way!"

— : You know how slow I am.

SHERYL SUTTON: By the way, New York writes as well. At twilight it is still drafting, with high pink letters. It writes, 42nd Street. It writes, 125th Street. But at midnight it is already working its way through the paper.

— : And at dawn?

SHERYL SUTTON: It casts its eyes over the sheet of paper.

CHAPTER EIGHTEEN

Sheryl figures things out and lectures – I answer, as best I can – Finally Sheryl has her say again

SHERYL SUTTON: Yesterday evening I read one or two of your essays which you gave me last time. *(Here Sheryl bowed, and wrinkled her forehead. She was sitting at the open window, so I could see at the same time her forehead, her face from the front and her back, her nape in the glass, as she kept on figuring out the periodicals in her lap. She cited my own former words.)* "Our fall reduced the reality of genesis to the unreality of mere existing," she quoted. "Since then art is *imagination's moral*, its contribution, laborious toil for the fulfilment, restoration of the reality, the incarnation of genesis. *Incarnate (Et incarnatus est)* – since then could be every masterpiece's concluding sentence, its authenticating stamp."

Do you think the same now, too?

— : Now, too. The gospel "writes" (I could also say: is crucified) between two words. One of the words is: "incarnate", the other word: "fulfilled". But the two words are one. And both are identical with the third, with genesis, with the foot-nail.

SHERYL SUTTON: "Much has been written on the kinship of mysticism and art. In fact the two are one in such a way that they are the complete opposite of each other. Two branches of the same road, the same love: ascending from the world and descending to the world, but in any case perfectly coinciding in the dynamic balance, the unexplorable peace of devoted obedience and liberated ecstasy. Jacob's ladder: with God's ascending and descending angels, the common and the only path of imagination finding its way home."

Could you say something more particular about this?

— : Let's stay with incarnation. Since our fall and our

expulsion from Paradise, the world goes on spinning and we go on being born and becoming incarnate. We become incarnate but not entirely. In some way or other nothing has filtered into our mind, will, imagination, our whole world. All at once we have become emptier and more cumbrous than necessary. This is why – at least on the level of imagination – a masterpiece, *from the fact* that it is incarnated (that is, with the laborious toil of imagination, will and the mind, has found its way back to original obedience) is again able to be free. To reach ecstasy. This is how the descending obedience of incarnation can be identical with the ascending trance of mysticism. Jacob's ladder.

Our failings, however, our sins are busily at work on the world's further deincarnation. Sexuality makes the body, richness makes what it possesses, more and more empty and depressing, meanwhile fronts get entangled one after the other. Art – we have spoken about this before – became envious of the certainty of science, then of the directness of streets.

SHERYL SUTTON: "When the soul is exhausted," you wrote, "and with it the imagination, we objectify the world somehow in style, the same way as exhausted love objectifies the other person in sexuality."

— : Later on, I think, I write about when literature strove for the certainty of science: it became stylistic, hermetic, narcissistic, it used the test-tube glass of science as a pocket mirror. It made a text of writing, "textualized" it. So no wonder that in due time it longed for just the opposite, for the monstrous directness of the street and of the city. In the test-tube it was no longer looking for certainty, which moved irremediably to the "mirror" (to "mirror literature"), but for directness, a hitherto non-existent interference.

SHERYL SUTTON: And do you find this so reprehensible?

— : Not in the slightest. I only wanted here to throw light on the fact that the drama of the imagination is one and indivisible, and not in the least the privilege of artists, but all people take part in it and mistakes perhaps hasten its denouement just as much as the appearance of some masterpiece or other. What's important for me is that art is only one of the scenes, and maybe not the most important one either, of the universal drama of human imagination, as unpublished works stand above published ones on occasion. (Hölderlin, Weil, Anton Webern . . .)

SHERYL SUTTON: "The God exiled from behind the facts bleeds through the tissue of history from time to time. The traces left on it are so endlessly undemanding that it is questionable whether we can ever get at it."

— : Yes, I wrote that, too. *(Sheryl was sitting so beautifully in the armchair now, like a cherub at a classroom desk. In her hands the periodical changed into a copybook, and my articles so serious that she only slowly and with difficulty managed to turn the pages.)* In my similes above – I carried on – I thought of the German camps in the first place, but mainly of those "undemanding" knocks and scratches which you know, too. When someone receives the host with belief, his imagination is forced to absolute "poverty", to a pictureless picture. Only this way can he believe that he is receiving God's body. That is why I admired Wilson for sentencing his actors, even those with star-movement, to clumsiness, awkwardness from the start, and like the fever-patient under the eiderdown, simply made his stage sweat. Imagination is the opposite of daydream images, as incarnation is of carnality. Wilson's theatre, even in its reconquered mirage, was beautiful again, for having remained undemanding throughout, and having obeyed something greater.

SHERYL SUTTON: I know now that in '67 I had a nervous breakdown, as I know of the Austrian woman from Linz that she suffered from manic depression. In her depressed phase she was sentenced to confronting herself, while in her manic phase to being irresponsible. *(Sheryl had put my text aside.)* From ourselves we can escape only in a hypocritical or in an exhibitionistic way. Or in both ways at once. In depression the eyes of the woman from Linz remained two holes, in which everything that could get in at all was annihilated. She could bear nothing from the world, but least of all that cruel confrontation which her illness forced on her. She was lying or sitting like the dog whose nose is held in his own dirt. Blessed are those who can manage all this in a contemplative way, keeping a certain distance.

Some wind of depression mixed with schizophrenia touched me too. Tenseness and helplessness at the same time: all the world's cruelty, the most burning core of which is still the sin that I committed. Pictures were bombing me from everywhere, worse than the world's torture, and harder than guilty conscience. They came from nowhere and still hit the mark. I knew they didn't exist (surely, experiencing true reality is finally always a very gentle thing), but it was impossible for me to stop them.

And the mock-marble sarcophagus? – So many kinds of words we know and use, then in a rare moment a word, which up to now has been green, ripens. The way one new word or another appears in a great poet's inspiration, which has always been there in his everyday speech and of course in the dictionary. I was hit by a fate, two fates what is more, with all their truth and lies, abomination and inhuman loneliness, when I *understood* the *real* just in what was *artificial* in it. And that *grey*, and that *stone veil*, and that *"unfamiliar man"* – have only helped me to push forward in what we call the artificial, but which in that moment gets as close to me as to a short-sighted person's eyes. I know it's an aberration, but since then I've been feeling that artificial materials accompany you further. The clinging of a synthetic nightgown corresponds to the last moments. True though, from real material we can learn more. But the other, the artificial goes further ahead with you. It is still with us, when the real is out of breath. How should I know? It sags from us, it keeps us occupied.

Then years later, when I had already been working with Wilson, the stage-hand takes me by the arm and tells me that he has a white rock to show me. He wonders, what do I think of it?

The rock stood in the middle of a hangar-like studio. It wasn't a rock, it was made to Wilson's order from some kind of foam. It was enormous, white and terribly light. Perhaps I could have lifted it with one arm, but my eyes grew tired just from this, at the first glance. Now I understood for the first time the hamstrung gaze of the woman from Linz, if something like that is possible. I looked up to the barred glass roof, and imagined that this rock would be on display sometime, and anybody who came to see it could break a piece off it for himself. The exhibition would come to an end when the rock was used up.

CHAPTER NINETEEN

Mr Környei the schoolteacher again – New York – Capitulation

SHERYL SUTTON: I didn't sleep all night. I brought a bottle of wine, but you can only have one glass.

— : Good morning, Miss Sutton! I didn't sleep, either. Would you please sit at the window!

SHERYL SUTTON: Your health, sir!

— : Your health, Miss Sutton! I wish you happy crocheting.

SHERYL SUTTON: Poor Mr Környei! He began to be regarded with suspicion first at Columbia, then in his hotel, and finally even in the street. Which is a rarity, though, for New York. But this small-town head with the crown of thorns of disorder! For days he didn't even move from his room. His shirt he still managed to tear off, but he could remember no more.

Waking up, he went down on foot from the twentieth floor. The stairs, like a gentle grassy slope, were covered with carpet all the way. Then softness ascended, and began to shine high above. Mr Környei entered an antique shop. It was four o'clock in the morning. Behind the counter perched an old woman.

"The hors d'oeuvre first!" announced Környei in firm tones, but the old lady didn't understand the hint. Környei already knew that *what he was looking for was here*. "The photographs?" he articulated, so the old lady pointed to the left and lit a cigarette.

Even the first photograph was news! Exactly what he was waiting for. A child dressed in his best directly under the wooden fence. "How peculiar this head is! Leaning back, and looking for a companion. I'm on the right track!" Then he lifted the book down. It was hand-written, and bound in leather. He looked into it and knew everything. By this time there were many people behind the counter. The whole family.

Környei put the manuscript back, asked for a light, and picked a face for himself from the family. As if drawing a card from the stiff pack: "Let's make a deal! I'll leave half of my scholarship here."

It was dawning in the street. Blue houses were swimming in pink. Környei went up to the twentieth floor barefoot. First he hacked off his tie with a razor, then took his dissertation and stuffed it out into the corridor. By then his chest was covered in blood, but the wound can't have been very deep. He knew what he was doing. He sat down and began to write.

– "What will become of me," he whispered, "God, what will become of me!" First he came out with the difficulties. "I know that I'm on the right track," he wrote, "but I can't see the continuation of the beginning even now. The beginning perhaps I can see, but not its continuation. How can this be?

New York has grown out of nothing, this is true, I mean the nothing, but what then? – Terrible that the man of old, the historian goes on and on meddling where he has no business to be! What shall I do? Shall I get drunk?

One thing is certain. Anything I put into words about this city looks frivolous. Sketchy. Or is it like that itself? Yes, the city itself is like that. And yet it isn't. On the contrary. No matter how monstrously it glitters, New York is a single candle-flame. It's there in the manuscript too: *'New York is a candle burning by itself.'*

I have to go about it carefully like the old photographers. True, this story which has no story is impossible for me to write. My whole upbringing, way of thinking, education are against it. But what if it happens to be the kind of story that has no vertical section, just a cross-section? But then, I even have the right, what's more, it's my historian's duty, first to introduce the personality who I can see before me with perfect clarity. When did he live, then?"

Mr Környei leapt up from his place, and took some sleeping pills. A double dose, and he followed them down with a drink, too. Then he locked the door on himself, which visibly calmed him. He sat at his sheet of paper again and continued.

"Yes, I could start with Captain Allen. Supposing?"

(Now Sheryl has put her knitting down, poured out and taken a drink, then found some paper and a pencil, and began to doodle playfully on her knees. She doodled reflectively. On her beautiful hand I could see at the same time what was irresistible, and what in a given moment could disillusion a lover.)

"From his very cradle George Allen was intended for the military profession by his folk, who were one of New York's oldest and most distinguished families.

Nearly from the moment of birth the child was nursed and raised by a black nanny. He only seldom saw his mother. He must have been five when an uncle of his from far away, holding him tight between his knees, on the occasion of a garden party, drew attention to him:

'So you're George?' The child nodded. 'Look into my eyes, sir, behave like a proper boy.'

At this moment George felt his mother's arms around him.

'What a sight your clothes are, sir!' But by the time she had fixed the child's frills, she had already forgotten it.

George went up to his room upstairs and changed his clothes. The black nanny had time off until the evening. The child sat about for a short while at the edge of his bed, then went down to the kitchen. But he didn't go in. Through the open door, from the corridor, he watched the servants breaking eggs, whipping cream in a copper cauldron, and having a good time tasting here and there. Suddenly he turned on his heels and ran back across the terrace to the garden.

By then his uncle had drunk copiously. A span of white cuff was showing from under his tightly buttoned jacket.

'George, it's you, sir!' he called out jovially. Then, embarrassed, he turned to George's father: 'I should like to warn you, sir. This child is extremely highly strung.'

By then George had a fever of nearly 104°. 'I'm cold, father dear,' he kept on mumbling, going upward on the wooden stairs. But at least his nanny had come back by that time.

He can't yet have been seven when he was packed off to military school. For the instructors his frailness was immediately striking. As if his laced boots were made of iron and his body of paper. His face knew only two kinds of state: a stabbing attention and a perfect absence. Later in military college one of his teachers made mention of this, in class too. To the obviously inquisitive question Allen replied with surprising roughness: 'I always pay attention, sir. But sometimes inwards, sometimes outwards. It depends.'

His gym teacher was the most baffled by him: 'He knows everything, he does everything. And yet he doesn't . . . I don't understand!'

His maths teacher, on the other hand, was admiringly enthusiastic. 'I have never had a student even remotely like him! Sometimes I feel I'm educating a Newton or Euclid. And, what's oddest, I haven't discovered any sign of self-importance or ambition in him.'

His chaplain hesitated:

'George Allen? Last year he was still thinking of becoming a priest after leaving school. Dogmatic. Dominican.' (About that time George had attained his sixteenth year). 'Now I don't even know whether he still believes. Reserved, a very reserved young man.'

'Otherwise is he satisfactory?' asked George's father.

'By all means,' answered the chaplain. 'For the moment he's interested in literature. Once I managed to have another talk with him: "Why did you give up dogmatics?" I questioned him. "Because it wants to reach certainty where that is not proper." "And literature?" "Literature is defenceless," came the curt answer. "And mathematics?" "Mathematics is an elegant man of the world! Which, of course, is not true," he added at once, and that was the end of our conversation.'

By then, though, the boy's father had already stood up, and took his leave hurriedly.

The eighteenth year of George's youth marked a turning-point in his life. It began with a hint tantamount to an insult which one of his class-mates committed against him: 'George, what a sight your Sunday best is, sir, like clothes sagging from a man dragged off to a reconstruction!'

George first took a long, searching look at the boy, then turned his attention inwards.

'Perhaps you're right,' he whispered. Which made no sense, since at school they had to address each other strictly with 'sir'.

'Allen, I will report you for offending me, sir.'

'Pardon?'

'I'm going at once to the officer on duty, understand, sir?'

'Come on, let's go for a walk. Please.'

From then on George went for walks now with this, then with another boy, in twos. Usually they strolled about in the middle of the gently sloping lawn, casting a long shadow on the grass, but staying in a rather narrow circle. Everyone who spent any time with him adapted to him, sooner or later. In class however, or on the sports ground, George became companionless again and again, even in the midst of the most uproarious laughter or the most overwhelming pace.

The teachers noticed the strange turn, how George got into more and more intimate relationship with the class in twos. What were they talking about? How did he make those who accompanied him conform to himself? Although from the way he moved, it was obvious that he wasn't striving for anything like that. On the contrary. Whoever he was walking with, it was as if two young mathematicians were absorbed in solving the same problem. At such a time, it didn't even matter that one of them was finer. George stepped up to a chestnut tree. None of the teachers could have heard his words. He slipped his head in among the leaves. The other boy did not follow his example. He stayed standing a yard from the tree, and boyishly grew heavy, then drew himself up.

At the end of the school year, to everyone's surprise, George Allen still did not part with the army, though he mentioned several times that he was hanging his uniform up, and going to university to study advanced mathematics. In the autumn we see him again at the opening ceremony of the military science school year. By that time his parents were getting divorced; they were living apart. In the course of the first year no special event happened to him, except that on speech-day he received almost all the prizes. On the ground-floor courtyard the assembled crowd meant the same as the summer heat. George hurried over to the post office and sent half the money to his old nanny. The other address is unknown to the present day.

His professors were fascinated, in the strictest sense of the word, by his capabilities. The daydreaming face could switch in a second from absence to unbearable, almost radiating presence. He made contact with several universities simultaneously, he was in touch with various departments, but never by word, personally, always in writing, by letter.

He was spending his second year at the Military Academy when again something brand-new came to pass. His philosophy teacher did not feel well, and requested George Allen, second-year academic, to take the class for him. The clothes on George Allen were really sagging now, as if he was at a reconstruction. Nothing was left, except his trousers. He stood like this for minutes, wordless. In the classroom an unknown silence grew, as in a remote forest. All elbows slid forward; somebody knocked something over.

George Allen's attention was fluctuating incalculably between the classroom and a kind of distance. A smile came to his face, and again he had arms, legs and smile; then nothing again. This eternal throbbing, which his words about Plato's philosophy had even intensified, was impossible to bear, to follow after a time. Most of them fell asleep in half an hour, others sat leaning back at their desks, like weary girls, and only one or two were still paying attention.

Then the bell rang, and after finishing his sentence Allen was about to go to his place. But stepping down from the platform, his legs refused to work. It wasn't that he fell. Like a bundle of rags, he rolled under the first desk. The boy who had wanted to report him brought him round. He was a kind, freckled boy, of whom George had said back in school: 'You would be the most beautiful girl, if you weren't cut from cardboard!'

'George . . .'

'Thank you, Carol.'

From this moment, I think, the steep rise of George Allen's career can be reckoned. From then on he was very rarely seen in twos, but much more on his own. By the age of twenty he was promoted to captain. His real activity however far outgrew his rank and position. The captain is a computer, those surrounding him declared, by which they weren't saying much. In the space of a few years George Allen created, almost unnoticed, the city's most enormous and up-to-date munitions industry and armed force.

At the same time – surprisingly – these were also his loosest years, which is hard for the historian to place. One morning he was found drunk in a bar. Another time he couldn't get home. Everything pointed to his being a solitary drinker.

In this period of his, he met Lenny Shinderman in a night-club. He invited the girl to his table, they stayed silent, then they went home.

'Wash your make-up off please, miss. While I'm making some coffee.'

When Miss Shinderman came back, the man understood everything. Everything on Miss Shinderman was white, so white that it was almost pink, that it nearly peeled and became abraded.

Light was never thrown on whether there was a relationship

between them. One thing is certain, Miss Shinderman always lived in the Captain's vicinity from then on, she became his secretary, his confidante.

'Miss Shinderman!' And the beautiful albino in her perishable perfection took a seat in the corner. (Much later, after Captain Allen's death, one or two sentences about the girl were found among some casual notes: 'Somehow she is oversized, like the surpassingly beautiful girl in the Grimm fairy-tale. That is why she eternally sheds and sloughs, why she crumbles and bleeds, that's why her feet had to be trimmed, so as to fit into the silk shoes, and this is why she is more beautiful than Cinderella.') A pencil in her hand, a notepad on her knees."

— : Sheryl, may I have another glass?

SHERYL SUTTON: Here you are, but have patience. Follow the good teacher's example.

— : I'm sleepy, Sheryl.

SHERYL SUTTON: Go to sleep then, I'll go on telling my story. *(From in front of the window, Sheryl moved over to sit at the end of my bed.)* How this teacher writes! Spectacles or a magnifying glass are needed!

Well: "George Allen has hardly turned forty, when he was unanimously elected the city's commanding officer. What did they expect of him?

Most people would break down at these kind of things. The form of address sags from the addressee. In New York an incredible silence has grown. Which of course needn't be taken at face value. Silence has grown the way it was there in the manuscript, 'New York is a candle burning by itself.'

The city's new commander replaced almost the entire headquarters staff and apparatus of power, and surrounded himself exclusively with young people. What is most odd however is that he compelled his circle of friends to go on calling him Captain. He was walking in twos again, as in his youth. It is regrettable that nothing from these conversations is preserved for us. Except the three days and three nights which

George Allen spent outside without interruption, hungry and thirsty.

But where did he wander, and what was he doing, then?

When he came back, he looked ten years older. He had breakfast on the terrace, in the company of one of his youngest adjutants. His hands trembled conspicuously when he spread butter, and put the knife down on his plate.

Yet the careful preparations began the next day. On the chosen day at the chosen time, George Allen stepped out onto the balcony. Down there the crowd blackened; a bird flew off, fluttered softly in the air.

'I, George Allen, the city's commander, in obedience to truth and the will of God, have decided that I capitulate. That all of us surrender. May the God of defeat speed us!'

In the endless procession Miss Shinderman marched beside George Allen. In the very front, a white and a black boy carried the key of the city of New York on a purple velvet cushion embroidered with gold. George Allen appeared before the public with Lenny Shinderman now for the first time. The girl was slouching along, but even like this the man was an inch or two shorter than her.

The girl turned her head aside. First to the left, then towards the captain. In the front the two boys paced with the key laid on the cushion, in their steps some hundred children dressed in acolytes' robes, with enormous flags leaning on the belts at their waists. Only after them came George Allen and Lenny Shinderman, then the officers' corps of the garrison troops, next in endless crowds the garrison and the city's inhabitants. They trod the marching songs and the church hymns underfoot, just as much as the silence which set in from time to time.

For long moments George Allen thought only of the girl. From now on he has to accept her. Also that she was cut from cardboard, and that her feet were crippled in her shoes. Why doesn't she let go, why doesn't she draw herself up? But then he was looking at the woman's face abraded from whiteness, and was no longer disturbed by his own high-cut general's cap.

In the city the car traffic had come to a perfect standstill, everyone had joined the procession on foot. It was getting on for six in the evening when they arrived at the foam-white power plants. Under the blinding, pored blocks of stone the flags could only inch forward. The blacks began a part-song. The distance and the hiding sun together braked the crowd. Captain Allen was tinder-dry and soaking wet. 'I'm asking for your hand, Miss Shinderman. It would honour me if you became my wife.'

The girl didn't answer. She was pattering along beside him gracefully and cumbrously, like a gull going for miles on foot.

In the meantime under the pored power stations the church flags couldn't stop bleeding to death. At that point Miss Shinderman sprained herself on a bump, and at the next moment the flags passed beyond the foam, and the key and the purple cushion grown heavy got out to the open field, under the open sky.

The general went ahead. The tired millions took their shoes off, stretched themselves out, and settled down on the grass.

George Allen from then on shared his waiting and his solitude with no one at all. But as night was falling, his face was all the more shadowed by the peak of the general's cap. In the two children's hands the cushion trembled, a moment more and they are falling headlong.

'Put it down on the floor!' George Allen ordered, folding his arms on his chest, then clasping them behind his back.

It must have been three o'clock in the morning. The actors were shivering in the neighbouring shrubbery, and were trying to lay a fire. The blacks became quiet. Everyone was here: the families and the private concentration camps, the half-breeds and the preening freckled ones.

'I wish to, and we must, surrender' George Allen kept repeating. 'This is what everybody wants, expects of me!'

In his long cloak he stood more and more solitary. Then there was only cap and cloak. Only coat. Shinderman stepped beside him. She said not a word, just stood beside him.

After six the sun first painted the sky crimson-black, then began to rise, beautiful and round. Everybody saw everything clearly. But first, they still admired the dewy grass. Only then turned round, backwards.

The skyscrapers were swimming in fog, and the fog was ruffled by wind. 'New York is a candle burning by itself.' Deep-crimson flag, with so many pictures in the middle.

In half an hour they saw that not everyone had left the city. On one of the Harlem balconies, a motionless man in yellow boots, red trousers and cornflower-blue hussar-type jacket. On a striped eiderdown a black woman with a yard of hair. Her grey locks were being combed by a lad, while the hard lights went out one after the other, and only softness went on turning and giving out light."

— : "Le monde existe, il est mauvais et irréel." (The world exists, it is bad and unreal.) "Dieu n'existe pas, il est bon et réel." (God does not exist, he is good and real.)

SHERYL SUTTON: This Weil-quotation is deeply true, I admit. And especially now. Still, it's one of those paradoxes that remain on the level of the intellect. The paradoxes of the gospel, however, pervade our whole beings, they hardly make us think. "Blessèd are they that mourn."

The fate of New York's capitulation was also determined by this.

— : Did they go back to the city?

SHERYL SUTTON: Mr Környei fell asleep over his sheet of paper. As far as the story is concerned however, beyond this point it's not too proper for us to pry further. One thing is certain. George Allen and Lenny Shinderman did not go back.

CHAPTER TWENTY

People and citizens – Icons – Why isn't the circus in crisis? – Fragment and sketch – It's raining

— : People in the field, on the balcony, and on the eiderdown. Only since my trip in May have I been able to see how long it is since I've been in New York *stylistically*. For example, one of my titles . . . *Big City Icons*. This title is neither Paris nor Rome, nor Budapest, nor Warsaw. Knowingly or unknowingly: *it was New York already*.

SHERYL SUTTON: But what about the icons?

— : "New York is a candle burning by itself." I would add: one piece of candle flame, which burns beautifully upright in front of an icon wall, even if it gasps for breath, even if from time to time it flutters.

SHERYL SUTTON: The icons are unchanged, and they don't move.

— : Only their tension, their intensity decreases or increases. While Western European painting got away from the heavenly kneeling-standing of the trecento to the motion-storm of the baroque, the icons didn't even stir.

SHERYL SUTTON: New York, for example?

— : Think of our own words. New York doesn't move either, but it throbs and bubbles all the more. Dream-citizens on the balcony, on the street-corner, on the eiderdown. Those who hurry do so without reflexes. The deep-crimson church flag full of pictures.

The exception perhaps was two art-nouveau corner houses grown improbably high. They reminded me of my childhood twins. They lived in Kaplonyi Street: two wilting, thin spinsters, grown very tall. They always went about in grey or dove-colour, always together, beside each other, strictly in line but always a slight way apart.

SHERYL SUTTON: It must have been like a circus spectacle.

— : It wasn't their height that I kept gazing at.

SHERYL SUTTON: It's not the acts in the circus that we admire, either. Think of the conjuror. He's cheating, obviously. But he must work unerringly, and undisguisably. Otherwise there's no sleight-of-hand.

— : And the others?

SHERYL SUTTON: There are more reasons why the circus is eternal, even if it's not attended, even if it has no public.

First of all: it's always doing the same thing, and with this satisfies the child-imagination in us. That, though we are curious, we always want to see and hear the same thing.

Secondly: perhaps even better than art, it has found the contrast of reality and illusion almost impossibly enlarged. It has a point where it can't cheat, where silence, continuous risk, profound attention, tiger tooth, bear paw or death-defying leap is its name. At the same time we can see beautiful girls, reckless muscles and liveried footmen. In short: we take delight in the inexhaustible street-organ playing, the changing of places of reality and illusion, danger and rashness.

Great directors and great artists have always attended circuses. Or at least reflected on their secret.

— : But if that's how it is, then what is it that keeps the theatre alive, and sentences the circus to homelessness.

SHERYL SUTTON: For the most part, social stupidity. Wilson didn't give his actors names, just as the most wonderful trapeze artist has no name either. Some kind of ancient greatness wants it like that. Despite its name, the Martelli trio is just as nameless as the sculptor of the Naumburg cathedral, or the stone-carvers of Notre Dame, or one village idiot or other into whose mind came the most beautiful lines of verse. Theatre must also become unsuccessful.

— : I'm glad that you like the circus too.

SHERYL SUTTON: With sympathy. As I do America.

— : And the stage?

SHERYL SUTTON: Most often in a critical way. When with sympathy, then I know that what I see is more than myself.

— : Modern art has very often experienced the insufficient. This is when fragments have come into fashion.

SHERYL SUTTON: This is over, I think. It's one thing when a perfect whole beneath the earth gets mutilated, and quite another when in the name of an unspeakable whole I create a fragment from the start. Such a thing is not only too self-important and modest, but prospectless too. The amputation of the fortuitous is unrepeatable.

— : And the sketch, Sheryl?

SHERYL SUTTON: The sketch, that's something else. The sketch, it's a circus. It's the kind of self-repetition and unrepeatable, non-recurring undertaking of an alert, trained to the utmost hand, attention and eyes that is enacted in a "moment", that can't be withdrawn, and is an entire unharmed and unharmable whole. In art – I don't know why – this is where we've got to today. At the same time this sketch must be worked out to the utmost. Not a worked-out play, a lemon-squeezer! A double salto, which is very slow, and in which the girl gymnast's youth and beauty is perfectly obvious. Well, to go back to the stage, the sort of sketch that, with its worked-outness, also informs one of those superfluous things which cause us to fall in love with someone, but from which someone can even fail in the first grade. The new theatre is illiterate. The kind of little boy who's perhaps only good for a ball-boy, but is happier and more *on the court* than the players.

— : That's why you brought up "gospel aesthetics"?

SHERYL SUTTON: Maybe. I don't remember. True, you or I were talking once about the unity that rolls at the bottom of great works. You hit the mark with your question. I didn't think it through. For me, in the neighbourhood of the ball that rolls in the depths, the Hellenistic and all other cultures are – either too gory, or too speculative, or they are based on harmony, or the hope of harmony, or on just the opposite.

Jesus is engrossed with the idea that we are one. God, man, tree, stone, everything. We don't, we shouldn't live in hierarchy or harmony. One day we'll roll and roll together, all of us, in the homeland which he promised.

It's terrible that it's still raining.

— : If it stopped, all the cinemas, theatres, galleries would be opened again!

SHERYL SUTTON: 99.4°. I don't understand your eternal slight fever.

— : Sheryl, your hands aren't oniony now.

SHERYL SUTTON: Don't be childish!

— : Sheryl, let's go to the circus sometime!

SHERYL SUTTON: All right. But I must say, I'm often very sad after the circus. Especially after the sideshows. And very hungry.

CHAPTER TWENTY-ONE

Sheryl announces that she has to go home – Walk and convalescence – Spring – Our last conversation and staying silent – Leave-taking on the kerb

SHERYL SUTTON: Tomorrow I have to go home. My mother called. Get dressed, it's wonderful spring! But put a coat on, all the same.

(Rue Rollin hardly managed to take the brightness in. Sheryl stepped beside me like a black cedar. My black winter coat was full of dust. First I tried to brush down the creases, then I found that winter coat, dust and convalescence go well with blossoming. What did we talk about? Nothing.)

SHERYL SUTTON: Are you really going to write our book down? Everything that we've chattered about?

(The sun stood over the top of the trees and over the Roman arena yawning in the middle of the garden.)

— : Sheryl, your hands aren't oniony now!

SHERYL SUTTON: Are you going to write the Easter down, and George Allen? The woman from Linz? The woman's arm hanging down with a handkerchief in her hand? My "dramaturgy?" Modelling?

— : I'll do my best to write it all down, Sheryl. Otherwise I'll go to sleep, too, with a handkerchief in my hand.

SHERYL SUTTON: I'll dig my hand under the eiderdown.

— : Would you like a cigarette?

SHERYL SUTTON: When I come back, I'd like to see you again. How dusty your coat is!

— : It's spring.

(Sheryl stood up, and left the park.)

SHERYL SUTTON: Hold on, I've got to buy something.

(I stopped on the kerb.)

— : Are you back already?

SHERYL SUTTON: Goodbye!
— : Goodbye.
SHERYL SUTTON: Goodbye, János!
— : Goodbye, Sheryl.
SHERYL SUTTON: Au revoir!
— : Au revoir.

The End